COASTAL CANDLELIGHT

MAGNOLIA KEY
BOOK THREE

KAY CORRELL

ZURA LU PUBLISHING LLC

Published by Zura Lu Publishing LLC

ABOUT THIS BOOK

Sometimes, to find yourself, you have to lose your way.

Amanda Kingston is at a crossroads. A successful event planner in the bustling heart of New York City, she finds herself burned out and yearning for something more. Seeking a break from the chaos, Amanda retreats to the serene, sun-drenched beaches of Magnolia Key, a place where time seems to stand still and life's simple joys take center stage.

She quickly finds herself entangled in the town's deeply rooted traditions—and in the lives of its colorful residents. At the heart of it all is the Magnolia Heritage Festival, a cherished celebration at risk of fading into memory without someone to breathe new life into it. Her plans for rest and relaxation are put on the back burner when she offers to help get the festival back on track.

What she hadn't counted on was her neighbor, the reclusive woodcarver Connor Dempsey, whose guarded heart and remarkable talent intrigue her. As Amanda's passion for planning the festival ignites, so does an unlikely friendship with Connor.

That is until she makes a decision in an attempt to help Connor that turns out terribly wrong. Then she gets offered a dream job back in New York. A job she feels she needs to take to pay back a debt to her grandmother.

Can the magic of the festival—and a little coastal charm—help them both heal from past wounds and discover a future neither of them imagined?

Coastal Candlelight is a delightful journey of self-discovery, the power of community, and the wonder of finding unexpected love in the unlikeliest of places. Dive into this heartwarming story in the Magnolia Key series, where every sunset brings a promise of a new beginning.

The Magnolia Key Series:

Saltwater Sunrises
Encore Echoes
Coastal Candlelight
Tidal Treasures
And more to come…

This book is dedicated to the magic in every sunset, and the promise each sunrise brings.

KAY'S BOOKS

Find more information on all my books at
kaycorrell.com
Buy direct from Kay's Shop at
shop.kaycorrell.com

COMFORT CROSSING ~ THE SERIES
The Shop on Main - Book One
The Memory Box - Book Two
The Christmas Cottage - A Holiday Novella
(Book 2.5)
The Letter - Book Three
The Christmas Scarf - A Holiday Novella
(Book 3.5)
The Magnolia Cafe - Book Four
The Unexpected Wedding - Book Five

The Wedding in the Grove - (a crossover short story between series - with Josephine and Paul from The Letter.)

LIGHTHOUSE POINT ~ THE SERIES
Wish Upon a Shell - Book One
Wedding on the Beach - Book Two
Love at the Lighthouse - Book Three
Cottage near the Point - Book Four
Return to the Island - Book Five
Bungalow by the Bay - Book Six
Christmas Comes to Lighthouse Point - Book Seven

CHARMING INN ~ Return to Lighthouse Point
One Simple Wish - Book One
Two of a Kind - Book Two
Three Little Things - Book Three
Four Short Weeks - Book Four
Five Years or So - Book Five
Six Hours Away - Book Six
Charming Christmas - Book Seven

SWEET RIVER ~ THE SERIES
A Dream to Believe in - Book One
A Memory to Cherish - Book Two

A Song to Remember - Book Three
A Time to Forgive - Book Four
A Summer of Secrets - Book Five
A Moment in the Moonlight - Book Six

MOONBEAM BAY ~ THE SERIES
The Parker Women - Book One
The Parker Cafe - Book Two
A Heather Parker Original - Book Three
The Parker Family Secret - Book Four
Grace Parker's Peach Pie - Book Five
The Perks of Being a Parker - Book Six

BLUE HERON COTTAGES ~ THE SERIES
Memories of the Beach - Book One
Walks along the Shore - Book Two
Bookshop near the Coast - Book Three
Restaurant on the Wharf - Book Four
Lilacs by the Sea - Book Five
Flower Shop on Magnolia - Book Six
Christmas by the Bay - Book Seven
Sea Glass from the Past - Book Eight

MAGNOLIA KEY ~ THE SERIES
Saltwater Sunrise - Book One
Encore Echoes - Book Two

Coastal Candlelight - Book Three
And more to come!

WIND CHIME BEACH ~ A stand-alone novel

INDIGO BAY ~
Sweet Days by the Bay - Kay's Complete Collection of stories in the Indigo Bay series

Sign up for my newsletter at my website *kaycorrell.com* to make sure you don't miss any new releases or sales.

CHAPTER 1

Amanda Kingston stood frozen on the crowded New York City street, unable to force herself to take another step. A flood of people rushed past her, bumping her shoulder and sending her annoyed glances to let her know she stood in their way. She backed up against the comforting solidness of a building and sagged against the rough red bricks. Her phone vibrated incessantly in her jacket pocket, each ding reminding her of the relentless demands on her time. A bone-deep tiredness settled over her. For a long moment, she simply stood against the wall, letting the city rush past her.

In that moment, surrounded by the city that never sleeps, she realized she was wide awake in a life that no longer felt like her own. Her life controlled her. She didn't control it. The phone dinged again as if in agreement.

The last event she planned had been a smashing success. Maybe too successful. It should have left her riding high on her accomplishments. Now people were begging her to become their event planner, inundating her with requests. Which was what she'd always wanted, wasn't it? A thriving, successful event-planning business in the heart of the city?

And yet, it no longer fulfilled her. The shine had worn off her dream. It had all boiled down to an endless stream of phone calls, tedious planning, and appeasing demanding clients. As the hubbub of the city swirled around her, she felt utterly adrift, questioning every decision that had led to this point.

As she pushed off the wall and turned toward her apartment, a taxi blared its horn, piercing the already deafening sounds of the street. A couple walked past, their hands entwined, but both talking animatedly on their phones, oblivious to anything going on around them. People avoided eye contact as they passed her. The energy and noise of the city wrapped around her like a wet blanket, strangling her.

She trudged up the steps to her apartment, took the elevator, and slipped inside, locking the double-deadbolts behind her. She had thought she'd really made it when she was able to move from her third-floor walkup to this apartment with an actual doorman and an elevator. A sign of the success she was making for herself.

The minimalist aesthetic and stark furnishings that she'd been so proud of when she bought them no longer seemed the correct choice. Oh, they were on point with current trends and the paint on the walls was last year's color of the year. But how had she ever thought this modern decor would suit her? The room was sterile and unwelcoming, not a beloved sanctuary to come home to. Her old apartment with its thrifted furniture, old, uneven wooden floors, and leaky windows had seemed more like a home to her.

She dropped her purse on the table by the door and kicked off her shoes, the noise echoing through the open-concept layout. She padded barefoot across the cool tile to the tall window overlooking the busy street, still feeling disconnected from her surroundings, from her life. Below, the street was packed with cars and throngs of people hurried down the sidewalk.

She had to make up her mind about which event to take on next. She'd been known to juggle two or three at a time as long as they weren't in the same week, her reputation for always getting the job done instilling trust in her clients. But recently, none of the requests had sparked one bit of joy for her. The thrill of coordinating the perfect occasion had faded with each new event blurring into the next in a haze of checklists and phone calls.

She crossed over to her small kitchen. The sleek stainless-steel appliances and glossy white cabinets felt cold and impersonal. She poured herself a crisp glass of sauvignon blanc and sank onto a chair, debating ordering in from the Italian place down the street or maybe just making a bowl of popcorn and calling it a night. Even boiling water for a simple pasta dish seemed like too much work after the sixteen-hour days she'd been putting in. A night of mindless TV on the couch sounded quite appealing.

The faded postcard on her fridge caught her eye and she smiled for probably the first time today. Magnolia Key. That postcard got stuck on every fridge in every apartment she had. A poignant reminder of going there with her family as a young girl. Before… well, before everything fell apart. When her perfect life had fractured into tiny pieces and been swept away by an unstoppable tide.

But still, those cherished memories of the two-week vacation lingered. The endless sunny days lazing on the sugar-white sandy beach. The evening walks along the old wooden boardwalk, her parents strolling hand in hand. The twangy scent of the salt air. The slower-paced, relaxed atmosphere. All those memories were something that no one could take away. It had been a magical time. Those small, simple moments could never be taken from her. She closed her eyes as images of the pristine beaches and turquoise waters filled her mind. She could almost smell the sea breeze and the heady fragrance of the tropical blooms.

She opened her eyes, got up, and walked over to the fridge, sliding the postcard out from under the magnet. Her interior designer had insisted that nothing be hung on the front of the refrigerator, but she hadn't listened to the woman. She ran her fingers over the faded photo on it. Her parents hadn't known, any more than she had, that their vacation to Magnolia Key would be their last one together.

She swallowed back the pain, the wound still tender after all these years, and put the card back on the fridge.

Exhaustion swept over her as she collapsed onto the couch with her wine, the relentless pace of her life in the city leaving her utterly drained. If only she could get back that carefree feeling of that time on Magnolia Key. The feeling of endless enchanted days stretching before her, brimming with unhurried hours and simple pleasures. Where no phones dinged. No emails demanded her attention. A time when her biggest concerns were finding the perfect shell or which flavor of ice cream cone to choose.

Frowning, she set her glass down on a coaster and grabbed her laptop. An idea began to form, a tiny seed taking root, giving her hope. Why shouldn't she take a vacation? When was the last time she'd taken one? She couldn't even remember. She could take a long one. Maybe for a month. Just the mere idea was a soothing balm to her jangled nerves.

She flipped open the laptop, her fingers hovering over the keys, and started searching. There—she found it. The perfect little beachfront cottage on Magnolia Key. Before she could change her mind or tell herself a million reasons why she couldn't do this, she booked the cottage. And not just for one month... she booked it for two. A shiver of anticipation and disbelief surged through her as she clicked on the confirm button.

She'd have to let her assistant know. Tell her assistant to handle inquiries and let people know she was unavailable for two months. Two glorious months! The luxuriousness of it thrilled her, a delicious indulgence she'd never allowed herself. The decadence of trading this noisy, chaotic city for the peace of the small quaint island town.

With a contented smile, she closed the computer and took up her glass. Raising it high, she toasted her daring decision. "To a much-deserved break."

CHAPTER 2

Amanda stepped into the brightly painted cottage she'd rented on Magnolia Key, inhaling the faint scent of lavender. A wide grin spread across her face when she saw the warm late afternoon sunlight streaming through the windows and the comfy decor that begged a person to come and sit down. Ah, such a refreshing change from her sterile apartment back in the city. She tugged her suitcases inside, then went back out and brought in a couple bags of groceries she'd gotten before she left the mainland. She closed the door behind her. Closed the door on her life back home and stepped into her two months of glorious vacation.

The last week had been filled with calls and

emails and clients begging her to take on just their one event, insisting she was the only one who could pull it off flawlessly. But she'd clung to her decision, politely but firmly declining. Her assistant had stood in the office, mouth wide open, when Amanda informed her of her decision to take two months off.

But finally, she'd packed up her things, flown to Florida, and rented a car. The ferry took her across to Magnolia. Memories of her first trip to the island had flooded her mind as the boat cut through the gentle waves. Standing up on the top deck of the ferry, holding her father's firm hand as the breeze buffeted them and they watched the island get larger and larger on the horizon as they approached.

This time had been different, of course. She'd been all alone without the comfort or presence of her family. But she didn't let the nostalgia curb her enthusiasm. She had eight glorious weeks spreading out before her, and she planned on enjoying every single sun-soaked day.

Turning her thoughts back to the tasks at hand, she put the groceries neatly away in the kitchen. Next, she tugged the suitcases into the bedroom, opened one suitcase, and decided to wait to unpack everything else. She rifled through until she found a pair of shorts and a cotton top. She slipped them on and headed out to the deck. It was almost sunset and she couldn't wait to catch her first one back on Magnolia.

The worn wooden planks of the deck were warm beneath her feet, and when she stepped onto the beach, she relished the contrasting coolness of the sand. She paused for a moment, drinking in the salty air and the last of the day's sunshine.

She wanted to throw out her arms and spin around like she'd done when she was a kid, but adults didn't do things like that. Feeling defiant, she scanned up and down the beach, searching for any onlookers, but didn't see anyone watching her. With a wide grin, she threw out her arms and spun in a dizzying twirl of circles. Her laughter mixed with the sound of the waves before she dropped down onto the sand, breathlcss.

Magnolia didn't disappoint with a magnificent display of brilliant colors streaking across the sky as the sun slipped below the horizon. A few stars flickered above her, tiny penlights in the darkening sky. She lingered on the beach, taking in every sight, sound, and smell. Cherishing the tranquil beauty of it all.

Finally she pushed up from where she sat and walked down to the water's edge, letting the waves slip over her bare feet and tug the sand out from beneath her with each surge. A lone bird swooped through the sky high above her, its call just barely audible over the waves.

She sucked in a deep breath of the salty air. Yes, this was just like she remembered it. The magical allure of Magnolia Key. The tension in her shoulders, a constant companion, started to ease.

As the evening darkened, she finally turned and went back inside her cottage, flipping on the lamps and filling the rooms with warm, cozy light. Yes, two months here was just what she needed. She settled into an overstuffed armchair, more at peace and content than she'd felt in years.

The next morning Amanda's eyes fluttered open, and she struggled to place where she was. As the fog of sleep dissipated and she finally remembered, a smile slipped across her face.

Magnolia. The start of her glorious two months filled with… nothing. No cell phones. No email. No demands.

Slipping out from under the soft sheets, she climbed out of bed and padded into the kitchen. Then to her dismay, she realized she hadn't picked up any coffee when she'd gone to the market. That wouldn't do. She needed her coffee. She hurried and changed into casual clothes—that in and of itself a great luxury. As she reached for the doorknob, ready to head out in search of coffee and breakfast, a burst of laughter escaped her lips. She turned and deliberately set her phone on the table by the door. No need for that annoying electronic pest.

She stepped out into the sunshine and decided she'd walk. The weather was perfect. Sunny skies and a light breeze that carried the faint scent of the fresh sea air. She headed toward the boardwalk, walking past the storefronts on Main Street. The quaintness of the town charmed her, each building adorned with striped awnings and large containers of blooming flowers lining the sidewalk. She swore it could be on a picture-perfect postcard, then grinned when she realized it was. Like the postcard back on her fridge at home.

Some of the storefronts looked like she remembered them, their fronts worn but inviting. A few were freshly painted in bright colors, adding a bit of vibrancy to the street.

She stepped out onto the boardwalk and let the sea breeze toss her hair this way and that. She tilted her face toward the sun and let it rain down on her, washing away her cares like the tide rushing out from the shoreline.

Her stomach rumbled to remind her she was hungry, and she turned to head back to find a place to eat. A charming cafe called Coastal Coffee beckoned with its cheerful teal awning and large pots of flowers on either side of the doorway. Coffee. Just what she needed. She pushed inside and gave her eyes a moment to adjust to the dimmer lighting.

A woman near the counter, her graying hair pulled back in a messy bun, waved to her. "Take a seat anywhere. Be with you in a minute."

Amanda nodded and scanned the cozy room. She spied a two-top near the back and settled into a chair. The place was full of customers enjoying their breakfast. The sounds of conversation and dishes clanking filled the air with a comfortable hum. The intertwined scents of freshly roasted coffee and tantalizing cinnamon wafted through the large, open room. Her mouth watered in anticipation.

The woman approached her table with a warm smile and set a steaming cup of coffee in front of her. "Coffee to start you off?"

"Yes. Please. That would be wonderful." She hoped it tasted as good as it smelled.

"The specials are on the board above the counter." She handed her a menu. "Blueberry muffins today. They're really good."

She glanced at the chalkboard and then at the menu in her hands. Everything begged for her attention. It all sounded yummy.

"I'm Beverly, by the way," the woman said. "I'll give you a moment to look over the menu and be back for your order." With that, she bustled off to take care of another customer, leaving Amanda to ponder all the scrumptious-sounding choices.

As she perused the menu, she sipped her coffee, savoring the rich flavor. She was in luck. The coffee was delicious. As she contemplated her choices, she overheard Beverly talking to a nearby customer.

"It's too bad about the Heritage Festival this year. I heard they might even cancel it," Beverly said.

"They can't cancel it. It's a town tradition going back decades." The older woman frowned, a look of total displeasure on her face.

"I know, Miss Eleanor, but after Judy took that bad fall, she's out of commission for a while, and no one seems to want to take over for her."

"Well, I would, but I'm scheduled to be out of town for a bit and someone would need to be in town this month to pull it off. It's only six weeks off." Eleanor tapped the table with two sharp raps of her fingers. "But we need to have someone run it."

"It would be a shame if they have to cancel it." Beverly sighed. "Anyway, let me know if you need anything else."

Amanda wondered what this annual Heritage Festival was all about. She imagined arts and crafts displays. Maybe a historical reenactment? Maybe food booths or even a baking contest? She reached in her pocket for her phone to search for information about it, then remembered it was back at her cottage. Ah, well. She'd look it up when she got back.

Beverly walked over and topped off her coffee. "Have you decided?"

"Yes, I'll have the blueberry muffins. And…

a side of hash browns." She handed back the menu.

"Great choice. Muffins are fresh-baked every morning." Beverly nodded with approval. "So, are you in town for long?"

"I am. A couple of months. Just taking a little break from… life."

"Ah, we all need a break sometimes, don't we?" Beverly smiled at her. "Well, come in here as often as you like. We've got great breakfasts and lunches. And if you're looking for dinner, try Sharky's. Lots of fried food and all of it delicious."

"Thanks for the recommendation." She appreciated the gesture of hospitality.

Beverly headed back behind the counter, leaving Amanda to her thoughts. It would be nice to feel welcome here and enjoy more meals at the cozy cafe.

The older woman Beverly had been talking to—Eleanor—stood up from her table, the legs of her chair scraping against the floor. The paper she'd been reading slipped from her grasp and fluttered to the floor. Amanda reached over to scoop it up and held it up to the woman. Eleanor's brow creased and her look was hard to read. Amanda couldn't tell if the woman was grateful or annoyed.

"Thank you," she said curtly as she snatched the paper back.

"You're welcome…" But her words trailed off because the woman had already turned and headed toward the door with brisk steps.

Beverly returned with her meal and set it on the table. "Here you go. Enjoy."

She ate slowly, savoring each bite, as bits and pieces of conversations swirled around her. A lot of chat about the weather. A few remarks about the festival. Not one person seemed in any hurry to get up and rush out. This is what she had craved, a chance to slow down and just enjoy the moment.

After lingering over a final cup of coffee, she paid her bill. "Thanks, it all was wonderful."

Beverly smiled. "Love to hear that. Coastal Coffee is my cafe and I love having satisfied customers."

"Well, you have one in me. I'm sure I'll be back soon." She meant it. She could already envision herself becoming a regular here.

"I look forward to it." Beverly's words held warmth, welcome, and sincerity.

Amanda threaded her way through the

tables and back out into the sunshine splashing down on the sidewalk. She squinted as her eyes adjusted and she settled her sunglasses on her face. The whole day stretched out before her, a luxurious expanse of unscheduled hours. Now, what was she going to do with it?

She had no agenda, no events to juggle, no emails or calls to answer. A heady freedom engulfed her. She was free to wander and explore and do whatever came to mind. With a contented smile, she strolled leisurely down the sun-dappled sidewalk.

CHAPTER 3

Amanda wandered in and out of the quaint shops lining Main Street. She couldn't resist the allure of the local items. First she purchased a soft, butter-yellow t-shirt emblazoned with "Magnolia Key" across the front. Then she chose a coffee mug with the words "come home to Magnolia Key" written in a pretty script in teal with an illustration of the island's iconic lighthouse on it. Armed with her purchases, she made her way back to her cottage.

She set the mug in the sink and hung up the t-shirt, smoothing the soft fabric, then wandered into the main room, settling onto an overstuffed chair. The chair surrounded her with comfort, and she picked up a novel she'd brought with her. Soon, she was lost in the book, a luxury she'd rarely had time for back home with the frantic pace she kept. When she glanced up at the clock a little while later, she was surprised to see it was mid-afternoon.

She got up and made herself a simple meal of a sandwich and a glass of iced water, which she ate sitting at a table by the window while enjoying the view. After cleaning up the dishes, she grabbed a hat and her sunglasses and headed out to the beach. Time for a nice, long beach walk.

The sunlight danced on the waves and a light breeze cheerfully accompanied her as she strolled along. Her feet sank into the warm sand with each step. She went down to the edge of the water and couldn't help picking up the perfect seashell here and there and slipping them into her pockets. She walked to the end of the island and turned back toward the cottage. As she got near, she cut up the beach, heading to her porch and relishing the promise of a cold beverage.

A large wooden structure beside the cottage next door stood with its doors wide open. It was a bit too nice to be called a mere shed. As she walked past, she glanced inside, her curiosity piqued at the sight of a man hunched over a workbench, busy at work.

As if sensing her presence, he glanced up and met her gaze. She squirmed uncomfortably at being caught staring but didn't look away. Instead, she pasted on a broad smile.

He rose from the bench and walked to the open doorway, pulling the doors closed behind him as he stepped outside. She caught her composure again and smiled warmly. "Hello there. I was just heading back to my cottage." She nodded toward the cottage next to his. "I'm Amanda Kingston. I'm renting the cottage for a few months."

She held out her hand, and he stared at it. His blue eyes remained cold and his expression guarded. After a moment, he wiped his hand on his shorts and took hers, shaking it quickly before snatching his hand back. "Connor. Connor Dempsey." His voice was curt and clearly annoyed at the interruption.

"Nice to meet you, Connor." She ignored his lack of warmth or friendliness. "So, this is your workshop?"

"Yes."

"What are you working on?"

He gave her a long look before answering. "Carvings. Wood carvings."

"Oh, that's so interesting." What a fascinating hobby. She was truly intrigued. She'd never met a wood carver.

The silence stretched between them as he seemed to contemplate his next words. "I prefer to work alone though. In quiet."

The rebuff was unmistakable. "Okay, I should let you get back to it." A twinge of disappointment crept through her. She guessed she wasn't going to make a friend of her neighbor. "I'm just next door if you ever want… company," she offered, keeping her voice light and friendly.

His expression remained impassive, and he simply nodded and reached for the door. "Need to get back to work." He disappeared inside and firmly tugged the door closed behind him.

She stood there for a moment, not sure if he'd hurt her feelings with his standoffishness, or if he was just some kind of elusive artist type that preferred his solitude.

Regardless, any hopes of becoming friends with this neighbor were dashed into pieces. With a small sigh, she turned and walked the few paces to her cottage.

Well, he was going to have to get used to her presence. She loved being out on her porch or on the beach. Determined not to let his gruff attitude dampen her mood, she made up her mind to be friendly to him if she saw him. She'd smile and wave but stay out of his way. Not even the grouchy neighbor would ruin her feel-good mood and the luxury of this vacation.

Connor peeked out of the side window of his workshop as his new neighbor headed back to her cottage. Thankfully, she went inside, leaving him in peace. He let out a quiet sigh of relief and walked back to the doors, swinging them wide open, letting in the sea breeze and fresh air. He hoped he wouldn't have to keep the doors closed up all the time to avoid the woman. He needed the natural light to work on his carvings.

What he didn't need was some woman coming by and constantly interrupting him. He didn't like anyone bothering him or infringing on his carefully cultivated solitude. That's why he made it a point to get his groceries promptly when the market first opened before many customers came in. Why he preferred to do any major shopping on the mainland where he was just one of many anonymous customers. He liked that. To just blend in so no one pestered him.

So the last thing he needed was this woman —what was her name again? Amy? Addy? A something. He'd already forgotten. He didn't need her constantly interrupting him.

Anyway, he'd seen her out on the beach last night at sunset. A time when he liked to stand in the doorway of his workshop and watch the sky as it changed. She'd better not wreck that time for him.

She'd been out there on the beach last night, spinning around like a crazy woman. Her brown hair tumbling in the breeze. A grown woman acting as a child.

How long had she said she was here for? Two months? He let out a groan. That was a long time to hide out in his workshop trying to avoid her. If she came by again, he'd have to set her straight. No interruptions. No distractions. Hopefully, she'd get the message.

CHAPTER 4

While the luxury of having nothing to do, no calls, and no meetings was a welcome escape from her normal life, after a few more days, Amanda was wondering what she was going to do to fill her hours. She'd finished two books, devouring them eagerly. Trying out recipes she'd found online also became a new distraction. One which required daily trips to the market, but she didn't mind at all. The cashier now greeted her by name, making her feel welcome.

She took her daily walks on the beach—and noticed the neighbor only had one of the doors to his workshop open. Which was okay, because she'd already written him off as a possible friendly face here on Magnolia.

She decided to head to Coastal Coffee for breakfast this morning. Beverly had been welcoming, and to be honest, she could use some friendly conversation. She was used to her days filled with people, and now she rarely spoke to anyone except for an occasional person when she shopped.

After strolling the short distance to the cafe, she walked inside, taking in the familiar ambiance and the scent of freshly roasted coffee that wafted through the cozy cafe. Her mouth watered in anticipation of her first cup of coffee of the day.

Beverly walked up and greeted her. "Good morning. Glad to see you again."

"Amanda," she offered her name. "Amanda Kingston."

"Glad you came back in." Beverly's words were filled with sincerity like she was truly glad she'd come back. "Just grab a table anywhere. I'll be right with you. Coffee?"

She nodded gratefully, took a table about halfway into the cafe, and settled into her chair. Beverly brought her a steaming cup of coffee. "Here you go. You getting all settled in? Didn't you say you were here for a few months?"

"I am staying a few months. And I'm mostly

all settled. Exploring around the island a bit. And I met one of my neighbors, but that didn't go well. He's rather standoffish. Apparently, he's a wood carver."

"Ah, Connor Dempsey. Good guy, but he likes to keep to himself."

"I got the message loud and clear that he doesn't want to be bothered."

"Don't take it personally. He's like that with everyone. Kind of a loner."

"I guess I'll give him a wide berth and let him have his space."

"He just likes his solitude, I guess. But, anyway, enough about the locals. You came in to eat. Today's special is oatmeal muffins. Very good. Or you could try our pecan waffles."

"Oh, the waffles sound good. I'll have that."

"Won't be long." Beverly's voice carried a warm, friendly tone as she headed toward the kitchen. Soon she was back and paused by the table as she waved to a woman coming into the cafe. "Tori. Over here."

The woman made her way across the room with graceful steps.

"Tori, this is Amanda. She's staying here on the island for a few months. Amanda, this is Tori."

"Nice to meet you." Amanda smiled at Tori.

"Nice to meet you, too. What brings you here to Magnolia?"

"Just taking a little break."

Tori laughed, the sound carrying a hint of wistfulness. "That's what I thought, and now I live here. Escaped the chaos back in New York City for a nice, peaceful life here."

"I'm from New York City, too."

Tori frowned and carefully studied her face. "Are you Amanda *Kingston*?"

She nodded.

"You planned the big gala for the grand opening of my play last year." Tori grinned. "Back when I was Victoria Duran."

"Oh, I didn't recognize you." Her gaze swept over the woman and her transformed appearance with gray hair and casual clothing. This Tori looked nothing like the glamorous Victoria with flaming red hair that she remembered.

"Not many do anymore," Tori acknowledged with a wry chuckle. "I actually bought the theater here in town. That's what's keeping me busy these days."

"Oh, that's wonderful. I have to admit I'm having a hard adjustment from the fast pace of my life back in New York to the slower pace here on Magnolia. Although the slower-paced life is just what I wanted." She laughed. "You'd think there'd be some happy medium, wouldn't you?"

"That's what I found with my theater. It's my happy medium. A way to feel fulfilled and engaged without the relentless grind of life back in the city." A contented smile settled on her face. "I love my life here."

"I'm glad to hear that. Would you care to join me for breakfast? I'd love the company. I just ordered."

"I'd be delighted." Tori settled into the seat across from her. "Beverly, I'll have the oatmeal muffin and coffee."

"You two get acquainted. I'll be back with your meals soon."

"So, how were your first nights here?" Tori's eyes held genuine interest. "I couldn't believe how quiet it was when I first got here. But now I can't imagine going back to the noise of the city."

"It was quiet. Although, I had my windows open and could hear the surf. So relaxing. Like nature's lullaby."

"So what are you doing with your event-planning business? Don't you have any events coming up? I heard you were really in demand."

"I'm taking a bit of a sabbatical. The fast pace, endless details, and constant demands on my time were starting to wear me down. I felt like I was losing the passion that first drew me to my career."

"I bet. You have a lot to juggle with all those details for each event. It can be utterly exhausting, I'm sure."

Beverly walked up with Tori's coffee. "Speaking of events. Did you hear that they might cancel the Heritage Festival?"

"Oh, no. I hope not." Tori's brow crinkled.

"They don't have someone to get it organized. Judy McNally was running it, but she took a bad fall. And Miss Eleanor is going out of town, or she'd step in."

"I... I kind of remember going to the festival when I was a young girl. I was here with my parents."

"You were?" Beverly asked. "Is that why you picked Magnolia Key for your vacation spot?"

"It was. I even have a postcard from here on my fridge. I've kept it all these years. I have such good memories of here."

"Magnolia Key has a way of getting to you,

doesn't it?" Beverly nodded knowingly. "It has a way of calling you back when you need it."

"I remember parts of the festival, but it was a long time ago. What all did it entail back then and what's different now?" Amanda asked. She couldn't help herself. An event planner wonders about these things.

"Well, lots of food. That's the same. Barbecue and fresh fish. And so many sweets." Beverly laughed. "And we have lots of music. Some small bands. A barbershop quartet. An arts and crafts sale showcasing local talented artists. And a display of exhibits and photos showcasing the town's history."

"I do remember the food. Cotton candy and funnel cakes. My father indulged my sweet tooth." The brief memory flickered in her mind of the soft pink spun sugar and her sticky fingers as her father led her out to hear a band play at the gazebo at the edge of the beach. She appreciated that not much had changed with the festival she so fondly remembered. "It sounds like the town really kept up the tradition over the years."

"We did. Though it has gotten a bit smaller over the years. And now it seems that no one wants to jump in and actually organize it."

Amanda clamped her mouth shut. *Do not offer to help. Do not.*

Tori sighed. "I could help out some, but I have another show opening at the theater and things are kind of crazy there right now."

Do. Not. Offer.

"It just is what it is. We're running out of time." Beverly shrugged, her expression resigned. "I'll get your food."

She and Tori sat and chatted while they ate their breakfasts. It was nice to have someone to talk to and share a meal with at a leisurely pace.

As they rose to leave, Beverly stopped her. "Come back anytime. For a meal or just to chat. You're always welcome here."

"Thank you, I will." Gratitude washed through her for the budding friendships she was developing in this town, and she was once again grateful for her decision to return to the island, if only for a while.

CHAPTER 5

Amanda rose early the next morning, eager to explore the island more. But first, she needed to get a few groceries. She quickly made a bowl of yogurt, fresh strawberries, and a sprinkle of granola on top. She knew better than to go to the store hungry. She'd come back with way more than she needed.

After breakfast, she headed toward the market with two canvas bags to tote her groceries back home with. As she approached the store, a familiar figure caught her eye. Connor. Mr. Leave-Me-Alone. He was loading groceries into his truck.

She eyed the distance to the door. Could she

get inside without him seeing her? At that moment, he looked up and caught her staring at him. Summoning her courage, she put on a bright smile and walked up to him. "Good morning, Connor."

He eyed her silently, and she wasn't sure he was going to reply. "Morning," he said curtly before turning back to load another bag of groceries into his truck.

She stood there awkwardly. "Lovely weather, isn't it?" She cringed that she was reduced to small talk about the weather. The man unsettled her.

"Guess so," he said as he closed the tailgate with a thud.

"I thought I'd explore the town a bit more today."

No answer.

"Any must-see spots you'd recommend?" She knew he wanted to bolt for the driver's door, but she couldn't help herself. She hoped her questions annoyed him as much as his non-answers did her.

"Look, lady."

"Amanda."

He nodded. "Amanda. There's the beach. The lighthouse. Or shops on Main." He paused, eyeing her. "Not much else to do around here."

"I see. Well, thanks for the suggestions," she said cheerfully, sensing his discomfort.

As an awkward silence stretched out between them, he shifted on his feet. She wavered between trying to continue the conversation or to just let him go and put him out of his misery.

Connor cleared his throat. "I should go. Lots to do." He moved to open the driver's door, passing ever so close to her as he did.

"Of course. I won't keep you." She stepped back. "It was nice to see you, Connor."

He paused, giving her a slight nod before starting the engine and firmly closing the door. As he pulled away, a tinge of disappointment crept through her. People usually liked her. She was a likable person, wasn't she? She was known to charm even the most cantankerous, demanding person in charge of the events she managed.

Obviously, that charm was lost on Connor.

She went into the store and got only the items on her grocery list. Okay, and a pint of ice cream. A woman needed ice cream sometimes, didn't she?

~

Amanda went back to her cottage and put the groceries away. She was half-tempted to take a spoon to the ice cream and indulge herself. Congratulating herself on her self-control, she headed over to the couch. She could go for a beach walk. Or maybe go see the lighthouse like Connor had suggested.

Or read. But she'd finished the last book she'd brought with her. There was a cute lending library inside Coastal Coffee, though. Maybe she'd offer up the book she'd just finished and see if she could find another one to read. Besides, Beverly had invited her to come back anytime, right?

She headed to Coastal Coffee and pushed inside. The now familiar sights and sounds of the cafe welcomed her. Beverly waved and motioned to her to take a table. She headed toward an empty table near the back.

"Just coffee," she said as Beverly approached.

"Coming right up." Beverly returned with the steaming mug. "No breakfast?"

"I ate early before a trip to the grocery store. Didn't want to go there hungry."

Beverly laughed. "Good idea. Otherwise, all this food that's not on the list just jumps into your cart, doesn't it?"

"Sure does." She held up her book. "I just finished this book and thought I'd leave it for your lending library. Mind if I look for something else to read?"

"No, of course not. That's why Maxine and I started it." Beverly glanced over at the bookshelf. "Maxine, she's my best friend, and she works here. I'm sure you'll meet her soon."

Just then, the woman from the other day—Eleanor—walked up to the table. "Beverly, you find someone to run the festival yet? We're running out of time."

"I… uh… I didn't know I was supposed to be the one looking for someone."

Eleanor frowned. "Of course you are. We all are. Otherwise, the festival will be canceled and we don't want that, do we?"

"No, we don't." Beverly agreed.

"I could help." The words came out before she had a chance to stuff them back in. But then, she had been wondering how to fill her days. And how hard could a small-town festival be to organize after all the huge events she'd run in New York?

39

"You want to help organize the festival when you came here to escape all that?" Beverly's eyes widened, and she turned to Eleanor. "Tori told me that Amanda here is one of the top event planners in New York City. She's highly sought after."

"And you want to help plan our little Heritage Festival?" Eleanor's eyes narrowed.

"I do." She shifted under the woman's unrelenting gaze. "I have… well, I have wonderful memories of the festival. I'd need help, of course. Someone to tell me what all you want for the festival. But then, I could arrange it."

"I'll help her. So will Tori, I'm sure." Beverly acted like she was waiting for Eleanor's approval.

The woman nodded decisively. "Okay then. It looks like the festival is back on track. I'll be gone a few weeks, but I'll see what I can do to help when I return."

Amanda didn't know why Eleanor's approval meant so much to her. She didn't even know the woman. But it appeared Eleanor had the final word on this.

"I'll have my coffee now." Eleanor turned and headed to the last table in the back corner.

"Better go get her coffee and cream." Beverly reached out and touched Amanda's hand. "Thank you for this. The town needs this festival. Some traditions are just meant to be kept."

CHAPTER 6

Amanda met with Beverly and Tori the next day, and her notebook rapidly filled with a growing list of things to do. Just like in New York. But this was refreshingly different. Not only had she picked up a cute notebook with seashells on the front instead of the heavy leather binders she used back in the city, but nobody was making demands or piling on pressure. Their appreciation was genuine, and their suggestions were offered freely. As she reviewed the checklist, the workload seemed surprisingly manageable, even with the short five-week timeline.

Luckily Judy, the previous organizer who'd been sidelined with an injury, had already nailed down a few musicians and food vendors. She'd need to get more options for food. And nothing had been done about the arts and crafts sale, but Beverly gave her the names of local artists, and they did have a small gallery on the island. She made a note to visit with the owner. Her mind buzzed with ideas and tasks.

After a few days of phone calls and meeting with locals, she realized not all the townspeople were on board with an outsider planning the festival. Even though she assured them that she wanted it to be just like she remembered from her childhood visit, they were skeptical. But she was determined to bring it back like it used to be or even better. Not everyone in the close-knit island community was convinced.

Beverly put up flyers in the cafe announcing the festival was on and took it upon herself to rally support for Amanda. She heard Beverly talking it up to her customers and saying that Miss Eleanor had strongly approved Amanda for the job.

Despite these efforts, a smattering of the locals were vocal with their doubts. She did her best to ignore it and tried to use her usual charm to win people over. Although it wasn't totally working…

She went into Coastal Coffee, hoping to see

a friendly face, someone who was actually pleased she was working on the festival. Beverly didn't disappoint. She looked up from where she was wiping off the counter and waved her over.

"Amanda, there you are." Beverly motioned for her to sit on one of the stools lining the counter. "I'm glad you're here. Now I can introduce you to Maxine. My very best friend since we were kids. Maxine, this is Amanda, the event planner I was telling you about."

"Oh, it's great to meet you. And Beverly told me how much you're doing to help organize the festival. I know we usually have an auction that will benefit the next year's festival so we always have funding in place. Are you still doing that?" Maxine's smile was warm and friendly. Not tentative like so many of the locals when they talked to her.

"We are. I only have a few items though. I'm afraid not all the townspeople trust me. But I can understand their hesitation. I am an outsider."

"An outsider with event-planning experience is just what the island needs to breathe fresh life into the festival. Don't you worry. I'll talk to some people and they'll all come around." Beverly's eyes sparkled with enthusiasm.

"And you can count on me to donate one of my pieces. I refinish furniture. I have this cute desk I'm redoing now. I'll donate that," Maxine chimed in. "And if I get enough time, I'll donate this small side table I found. It needs a lot of work, but I bet I can finish in time."

Beverly slid a piece of pecan pie over toward her. "Here, on the house for all your hard work. How about some coffee with that?"

"Thank you." She picked up her fork and took a bite, savoring the rich buttery flavor and the flakiness of the crust. "Oh, my. This is the best pecan pie I've ever tasted."

"Get it from Julie over on Belle Island. She does all our baked goods. I get them delivered daily on the first ferry of the day."

"Well, Julie is a master at her craft. I've been trying out some new recipes with my free time, but I'm sure not up to this caliber. I burnt the crust edge on an apple pie a few days ago. I'm going to try again, though."

"Absolutely. And if you perfect something, you can enter it into the baking contest at the festival."

Her fork froze midway to her mouth. "The baking contest? Did we talk about that?" A hint of panic crept through her.

"Didn't we? Well, don't worry. I'll put a signup sheet here at the cafe. We'll get lots of entries. We'll just need a judge or two from out of town to keep the judging impartial."

Amanda opened her ever-present notebook and jotted down a note about the baking contest, her pen scratching across the page. She frowned, hoping she hadn't forgotten something big that everyone would be expecting.

"Oh, and I contacted Heather Parker. I'm friends with her mother, Evelyn. She's from over in Moonbeam. She's going to show a couple of her illustrations at the arts and crafts show." Beverly smiled. "It pays to have friends with talented daughters."

Amanda looked up from her notebook, relief washing over her. "Thank you so much. I haven't gotten very far with people entering the show."

Beverly's eyes brightened. "You could ask Connor."

She hesitated, recalling her somewhat unpleasant encounters with him. "I don't know... He was very clear that I shouldn't bother him."

"Well, if you run into him, you could at least ask. It wouldn't hurt. He does wonderful wood carvings, though I haven't seen one in years. He used to sell them around town, but not anymore. Not sure where he sells his work."

"Maybe. If I just happen to run into him." And if he'd even talk to her. Which she doubted.

"Connor who?" Maxine asked.

"Connor Dempsey. He came to town while you were away. I think he's been here about eight or so years now."

"Hm, haven't met him."

"He doesn't get around much. I don't think he's ever been into Coastal Coffee." Beverly shrugged. "Kind of a loner."

Amanda finished every single bit of her pie, relishing each decadent, flakey bite as they chatted about the festival. She finally rose to leave. "I really appreciate your help. Both of you."

"No problem. We're glad to help." Beverly took the empty plate. "Just ask if you need anything at all."

"And thanks for helping with the festival. I'd hate for Magnolia not to have it after all the years it's been an annual thing." Maxine came out from behind the counter and waved to a customer. "You're really a godsend to this town and the festival."

Amanda walked out of the cafe feeling much more positive than when she'd entered. She could do this. She'd show Magnolia the best Heritage Festival they'd ever had.

Beverly and Maxine cleaned up the cafe after closing, carting the last of the dishes to the kitchen and starting up the dishwasher. "You got time for some tea?" Beverly asked. "It feels like ages since we've had much time to chat and catch up."

"Sure, I have time. I'm just headed over to Second Finds this afternoon. And I think Dale and I are going to have dinner at his place afterward."

Beverly poured them both large glasses of tea and handed one to Maxine. They sat down at a small table in the corner of the kitchen. "So, it seems like you and Dale are getting along fine. Seems like someone is always telling me they saw the two of you somewhere."

Maxine laughed. "We do a lot together, I admit. Then he sells my refinished furniture pieces at his shop so there's all that time when we're out scouting new pieces for his store or for me to refinish."

Maxine's eyes lit up when she talked about Dale. Beverly couldn't be happier for her friend. She deserved someone like Dale. Someone who appreciated her.

Beverly paused, then plunged on. "I almost hate to ask… but how are things with you and your kids? Did Tiffany ever forgive you for not moving back and taking over the care of her baby?"

Maxine's expression darkened and sadness crept into her eyes. "I haven't heard a word from her. I've emailed and texted. No answer. But knowing Tiffany, she'll get over it when she needs something."

"And your son?"

"Not a word. No, he did send me a long scathing email about what a disappointment I am." Her voice faltered slightly.

She reached out and took Maxine's hand. "Don't listen to either of them. You're a wonderful mother. They are just…" She caught herself before she said they were spoiled brats. But they were.

"They just… expect things to be how they

want them to be. They've never had to work very hard for anything in their lives," Maxine said, her voice full of frustration. "It's partly my fault. I spoiled them and did everything for them."

"But they're adults now. They need to learn to take care of themselves."

Maxine let out a long sigh. "I know. They do. I just hope they'll come around soon. I would love to be there for the birth of the baby."

Beverly fumed silently. It would be just like Tiffany, with her stubborn and vindictive nature, to deliberately withhold the news of the baby's birth, simply out of spite. Maxine deserved so much better from her ungrateful children.

Maxine picked up her tea, the ice rattling in the glass. "Anyway, let's change the subject. Any more news on Cliff's plan to build the high-rise at the end of the boardwalk?"

"Not that I know of. I haven't seen Cliff except for one time at the end of the street. He was talking to his mom. And Miss Eleanor was chewing him out." Beverly relished the sense of satisfaction of Miss Eleanor putting Cliff in his place. "I turned right around and hurried away.

I have no desire to run into him again. Or speak to him."

"I heard there's going to be another town meeting about it soon."

"That's what I heard. When we find out the date, we'll make sure that everyone shows up. We'll show Cliff that's not what we want for Magnolia." Not that she thought Cliff cared one bit about what Magnolia wanted. He'd left Magnolia behind all those years ago. Left *her* behind. A hint of bitterness stabbed her every time his name was mentioned. Now she didn't want anything except for him to leave town again.

"Well, if Miss Eleanor gets her way—and she usually does—her son doesn't have a chance." Maxine grinned. "She'll send him packing, which is just what we need."

They clinked their glasses and toasted Cliff's departure.

CHAPTER 7

Connor stood at the window of his cottage, watching the storm rage outside. It had come in abruptly, giving him barely enough time to close up his workshop and get back to the cottage.

Lightning crackled in the sky, illuminating the crashing waves on the beach. The lights flickered, and he held his breath, hoping they wouldn't go out. His hopes were in vain because his cottage plunged into total darkness. He grumbled under his breath as he headed to the cabinet with the lantern and flashlights. Who knew how long the electricity might be out?

He glanced out the window and over to that Amanda woman's cottage. It was in total darkness, although he knew she was home. He'd seen her hurry up the beach to her cottage right before the storm rolled in. She probably didn't even have enough sense to have storm supplies. Flashlights, food that didn't need to be cooked, extra water.

As much as he wanted to ignore the dark cottage next door, his conscience nagged at him. His instinct to avoid any and all interaction with his new neighbor warred with a sense of unease at the thought of her alone in the dark during the storm.

His conscience won. With a deep sigh, he went to the closet and took out his raincoat. He grabbed some candles, matches, and an extra flashlight lantern. Hoping she wouldn't take this as an overture toward friendship, he opened the door, bracing himself against the buffeting winds and pelting rain. Holding up the lantern to light his way, he sprinted the short distance to her cottage and climbed the porch stairs, grateful for the overhang over the front door for meager protection against the elements.

As he paused there, irritation at this deviation from his habit of avoiding people poked at him. Why should he care if some city person didn't know enough to prepare for storms?

Connor Dempsey. Mind your manners. We were raised better than this. He swore he could hear his older sister's voice chastising him.

"I hear you, Megs," he said under his breath.

He rapped briskly on the door and then waited for Amanda to answer.

What was taking her so long? He scowled and knocked again, this time harder. Maybe she couldn't hear him over the noise of the storm?

Well, if she didn't answer, there wasn't much he could do, now was there? He turned to leave, then sighed, still hearing Megan's voice. Turning back once more, he pounded on the door this time and called out her name. "Amanda? You in there? It's Connor."

"Come in."

He barely heard her over the storm. He tried the door handle and found it unlocked. He stepped inside, dripping water on her floor, and swept the lantern high, illuminating the room.

Amanda lay on the floor. His heart did a double-beat, and he crossed the distance in two long strides. "Are you okay?"

"Yes, I just tripped over the coffee table when I was trying to find my phone so I'd have some light to look for flashlights or candles."

He knelt beside her. "You sure you're okay?"

"Yes. Really. I am."

He stood up and reached down a hand. She hesitated slightly, then grasped his hand as he pulled her to her feet. She stood unsteadily for a moment, then regained her balance.

"So you came to check on me?" She tilted her head to the side, eyeing him with a bit of skepticism.

"Saw it was dark over here. Wasn't sure you had storm supplies. Sometimes when the island loses electricity, it takes a while to come back on."

"I'm not sure if there are flashlights here or not."

"I brought you some." He set the lantern down and pulled two flashlights out of his pocket. "And candles and matches. But be careful with those. Don't leave them unattended." Last thing he needed was for his neighboring cottage to burn down.

She rolled her eyes at him. "Of course I wouldn't leave them unattended. Give me some credit."

He set the flashlights, candles, and matches on the table. "So you're good?"

"Yes, I'll be fine. Thank you for the

flashlights. If I find some here, I'll return yours right away."

"Don't be going out in this storm. It's not safe."

"You went out in it."

He let out a long sigh. "Because I thought it was the right thing to do to check on you."

"Well, it was very kind of you."

He shrugged awkwardly, wanting to make his escape.

"Can I repay you with a hot cup of coffee? I'd just finished making it when the lights went out."

As much as he was tempted by a hot drink, he didn't really want to stay.

"Please, it's the least I can do to thank you."

Without waiting for him to say yes, she grabbed a flashlight and headed to the kitchen, then promptly returned with two mugs. He couldn't really say no now, could he? He shrugged off his raincoat and hung it on a coat rack by the door. She pressed a mug into his hand. They stood there awkwardly, the silence between them roaring louder than the clashes of thunder outside.

She turned and set her mug down on the

coffee table. "I'm going to look for flashlights here."

She returned with candlestick holders. "Found these." She put the candles in and lit them. A warm glow surrounded them.

She turned toward the couch. "Come. Sit down."

Once again, she didn't wait for an answer and that annoyed him, but he did what she said. She sat on the couch and he sank into an armchair across from it.

"You got things to eat if you can't cook?"

"I do. Crackers and cheese. Some fruit. Um… well, I'm sure I have other things."

He should offer to let her come over for food if she ran out, but he wasn't ready to make that suggestion just yet. He'd wait and see how long the electricity stayed off. He took a sip of coffee. It was surprisingly good. Not some run-of-the-mill coffee from a can.

"It's good. The coffee, I mean."

"Thank you. I bought some ground coffee beans from Beverly at Coastal Coffee. You know her, right?"

"Kind of." It was more like he knew *of* Beverly. Everyone did. But he didn't go to her cafe or anything. He preferred to eat at home.

But he did know most of the locals. At least who was who. Not that he was really friends with any of them. He liked his solitude. Liked it a lot.

"Beverly and her friend Maxine are helping me with the Heritage Festival. I took over organizing it."

He narrowed his eyes. "Why'd you do that?"

"Because they needed help and I have experience planning events."

"But you're not even from here."

"But I have fond memories of going to the festival with my parents when I was young. I'd hate to see it end just because they didn't have someone to run it this year."

"Seems like a strange way to spend your vacation time." He shook his head.

"I'm kind of enjoying it. It was a hard adjustment from being so constantly busy in New York to just having all this time on my hands here in Magnolia. Besides, Beverly and Maxine and a lot of people are very grateful for my help." She shrugged. "Not everyone. Some are as skeptical as you are."

"Still think it's strange for an outsider to plan the event."

"That's what event planners do. Plan events.

That's what I do for a living." She flashed her eyes at him. "And I'm very good at what I do."

Her eyes were filled with determination. That was easy to see, even in the light from the candles.

"If that's how you want to spend your time. Still seems strange to me." He shrugged.

"It is what I want to do. And I'm meeting people around town and…" She shook her head. "Never mind. I know. You like your space." She stood. "Thanks for the flashlights and candles."

He swallowed the last of his coffee, wishing he could ask for a to-go cup, and handed her the mug.

She followed him over to the door and he slipped his raincoat back on. "Mind those candles," he said as he left.

It took every ounce of Amanda's self-control not to slam the door behind Connor as he left. The nerve of the man, treating her like some clueless, incompetent twit. Did he honestly believe she needed a lecture on candle safety?

She'd been planning events for years—

complete with candles—and knew exactly how to handle a few decorative flames. And his dismissive attitude about her running the festival? Completely uncalled for. She didn't need that either. He was just another skeptic. She'd had enough of them.

Determination surged through her. She'd show all of them, Connor Dempsey included. She would. This Heritage Festival would be the most spectacular one the town had ever seen. She'd show them firsthand exactly what Amanda Kingston was capable of achieving. She'd pour everything she had into this festival, leaving no detail overlooked, until even the most stubborn doubters would have to acknowledge she was good at her job. Including Connor.

She went to the kitchen to get another cup of coffee, savoring the comforting aroma. Might as well enjoy it while it was still warm. Who knew when she'd be able to brew another pot? The warmth from the mug seeped into her palms as she took the coffee back to the couch and settled onto it, curling her legs beneath her.

She glanced at the flashlights and extra candles he'd brought over for her. That was such a nice, neighborly thing to do. Although she could tell he was irritated that he'd done it. Like it actually pained him to do something nice for someone.

Whatever. That Connor Dempsey was the most infuriating man. She probably should have asked him to show some pieces in the arts and crafts show like Beverly suggested. But somehow, she was certain he would have said no. His standoffish—bordering on rude—manner made it clear he wasn't much interested in participating in community events.

Fine. They'd have the show without his carvings. They didn't need them. She'd find other artists willing to show their work. She snatched her notebook off the table and jotted some notes.

She'd showcase other local artists and bring the community together with a festival the likes of which they'd never seen.

She'd show Connor she was good at her job. She'd show everyone.

CHAPTER 8

Thankfully, the storm was over when Amanda got up the next day, and just as she was despairing the lack of hot coffee, the electricity came back on. She made a pot and then hammered away at her to-do list.

Things were starting to come together for the festival. She should never have let some of the naysayers—and Connor—let her doubt herself. The musicians were booked. She'd rounded up plenty of food. Even found a funnel cake vendor to come. She couldn't leave that detail out after her fond memories of having one with her father.

The perfect reward for all her efforts was a long beach walk. Afterward she planned to pour herself a glass of wine and read the book she'd picked up from Beverly's lending library.

The fresh sea air invigorated her. She headed toward her cottage after finishing her walk. Connor stood just inside his workshop, the doors wide open. She hesitated and debated whether to stop and say hi. He'd made it perfectly clear he preferred to be left alone, despite his neighborly gesture yesterday.

Before she could decide, a little girl darted past her, her dark curls bouncing with each step. The girl's face lit up with pure joy when she spied Connor.

"Uncle Connor!" The girl launched herself into Connor's arms, and he scooped her up, a genuine smile transforming his face. Well, that was a first. She'd never seen the man smile.

Amanda watched him, surprised by the warmth and affection in his expression. He looked so… happy.

The little girl looked over at her and wiggled out of Connor's arms. "Hi, I'm Brooklyn. Are you Uncle Connor's friend?"

Amanda glanced at Connor, unsure how to respond. His smile faded, replaced by the same guarded expression she'd grown accustomed to seeing. Her brief glimpse at his unexpected softer side vanished as quickly as it had appeared.

"I'm Amanda. I'm staying next door." She gestured toward her cottage.

Brooklyn skipped over to her and looked up, her eyes filled with excitement. "Have you seen Uncle Connor's carvings? They're aaaa-mazzzzz-ing. You have to come see them." Brooklyn tugged on her hand.

A woman with the same dark hair as Brooklyn's approached, a warm, friendly smile on her face. "Hi, I'm Megan. Connor's sister. And that little whirlwind is my daughter, Brooklyn."

"Hi, Megan. Nice to meet you."

"Please, go ahead and take a look. My brother is incredibly talented, even if he's too modest to admit it." Megan nodded toward the workshop.

Connor shifted his weight, his discomfort evident. "Megs, I don't think—"

"Nonsense." Megan waved her hand dismissively. "Your work deserves to be seen and appreciated."

Brooklyn tugged on Amanda's hand insistently. "Come on, I'll show you!"

She looked over at Connor who shrugged slightly and nodded, if very reluctantly.

Amanda let herself be led into the workshop. As she stepped inside, her breath caught. The workshop was lined with shelves full of intricately carved pieces—birds in flight, dolphins leaping out of waves, a sea captain in a rain jacket, and even some replicas of local landmarks.

"Oh, Connor. These are… magnificent. I've never seen anything like them. You are so very, very talented."

"That's what I keep telling him," Megan said as she hip-checked her brother.

Connor shrugged. The very shrug of his that was beginning to annoy her. "It's just a hobby of mine."

"This is not just some hobby… It's art. It's beautiful. It's… remarkable." She could barely stop the flow of praise.

Megan shook her head. "He's always so modest about his work. He really is talented, isn't he?" Sisterly pride shone in her eyes.

Taking a deep breath to gather her courage, she turned to him. "Connor, you should put some pieces in the art show at the festival."

"No." His answer came quick and firm.

"But—"

He held up a calloused hand, his jaw set. "I said no."

Megan let out a long sigh and exchanged a look with Amanda that spoke volumes about her brother's stubbornness. "Connor, you should. Your work deserves to be shown. I don't know why you keep it all locked up here in your workshop."

Connor's eyes flashed with frustration. "Megs, I'm not going to argue with you about this. Just drop it. Please?"

"Hey, Uncle Connor, let's go shelling." Brooklyn grabbed Connor's hand and tugged, interrupting the confrontation. "You promised we would next time we came to visit."

"Sure thing, princess. Let's go shelling." He grabbed a bucket from the workshop and slipped past Amanda and Megan, looking grateful for a reason to escape. "Be back soon."

Amanda turned to Megan. "Well, it was worth a shot. He's pretty stubborn when he makes up his mind, isn't he?"

"Most stubborn man to walk the earth. Good thing I love him and he's a fabulous brother and uncle."

"I was just going to pour myself a glass of

wine and sit on my deck. Would you like to join me while you wait for Brooklyn and Connor to get back?"

"I'd love to."

They walked to her cottage, and she poured them glasses. They settled onto the plump cushions on the wicker chairs.

"So, the town is having an art show?" Megan asked as she stretched out her legs.

"It's part of the Heritage Festival. I was hoping Connor would show some of his work. But I think that was a pretty firm no."

"He rarely changes his mind once it's made up. I'll work on him some, but I can't make any promises."

"I'm helping plan the festival and I do need some more local art for the show."

"How long have you lived here on Magnolia Key? I don't remember meeting you before."

"I don't live here. I'm just here for a few months. Taking a break from real life." She held up a hand. "And I know what you're going to say. Why am I working on the festival then?"

"No, I think it's great that you are. Honestly, I couldn't just sit around doing nothing for a few months."

"I'm an event planner by trade, so it made

sense to jump in and help. And I've made some good friends here on the island already. Though some townspeople aren't thrilled with an outsider being in charge. And Connor thinks I'm ridiculous for doing it."

"Connor's bark is worse than his bite. He really is a sweetheart under all the gruff exterior of his."

"If you say so." She still was skeptical.

"He's not much of a joiner, so he probably can't understand why you'd want to head up the event." Megan took a sip of her wine.

"I'd love to see the festival get back to what it used to be. I went to it with my parents when I was a young girl. I still have such great memories of it and of the island."

"Are they coming to the festival this year?"

"Ah… no." Amanda's voice caught. "They… they passed away when I was young."

"Oh, I'm so sorry. That's so hard. I know how hard it is. Connor and I lost our parents a long time ago too. I was in college and Connor was just finishing high school. It was rough going for a while."

"I'm sorry for your loss too."

"So, who did you live with after your parents died?"

"First, I lived with my grandmother. It was nice. She helped me get through it all. But then… she developed Alzheimer's." She looked out at the water for a moment as emotions crept up on her, then turned back to Megan. " I tried to take care of her, but I was so young. My family finally said I had to move out, and they put her in a memory care unit. I was heartbroken. It was like losing my parents all over again. Then I was kind of passed around from family member to member. Lived with my aunt and cousins for a bit. Then another uncle. Went to college with the money I inherited, moved to New York City, and became an event planner. That's my life in a nutshell."

"Must have been hard losing your grandmother, too, and moving around like that." Megan's eyes were filled with empathy. "We at least were old enough to live on our own. I had an apartment at college, and Connor moved in with me. He worked odd jobs and then started up with his wood carving. He had quite a bit of success with it."

"So why did he move to Magnolia?"

"I'm not sure why he picked it. I teased him it was because it's so hard to get here. Have to take the ferry and everything. But I try to bring Brooklyn as often as I can. She adores Connor."

"Looks like he adores her too."

"Brooklyn has him wrapped around her little finger. He'd do anything for her."

Just then, Connor and Brooklyn came back from their shelling adventure. Megan stood up. "Thanks for the wine. I should go. I promised to cook my world-famous mac and cheese to go with the burgers Connor is grilling." Her eyebrows shot up. "Oh! You should join us."

Amanda shook her head. "Thanks, but I'll let you all have family time."

"You sure?"

She nodded. Megan walked down the stairs and trotted over to Connor's. Brooklyn danced around the two of them and pulled shells out of the bucket, proudly displaying them to her mother.

Connor looked over toward her deck one time, his gaze lingering for a moment before turning back to Brooklyn and scooping her up in his arms.

One thing was certain. Connor Dempsey was a complicated man.

CHAPTER 9

The next morning Amanda headed to Coastal Coffee. She'd gotten into the habit of going there for breakfast two or three times a week. As much for the company as the delicious food. A bit of a sense of belonging washed over her as she waved to Beverly and took a table near the front where the sunlight filtered in through the windows. The aroma of freshly baked pastries made her mouth water.

Glancing at the chalkboard above the counter she saw that blueberry muffins were today's special. Now she was torn between the pecan waffle—always one of her favorites—and the muffin. Or, she could go with the healthier yogurt, fruit, and granola.

Beverly brought her over a cup of coffee.

"Morning. Looks like you're becoming a regular."

"I guess I am. I'll have…" She frowned, trying to make up her mind between the tempting options. "Okay, the blueberry muffin. And a side of the yogurt." That almost made her feel better about the calorie-laden muffin.

"Good compromise." Beverly's eyes twinkled with amusement. "Back in a flash."

Tori came in and hurried over to her table. "Oh great, you're here this morning. I've been wanting to catch up with you and hear all about the festival. Mind if I join you?"

"Please. I've just ordered."

Tori sat down and placed her order. They both sipped their coffee as Amanda told her all the things she'd accomplished with the festival planning.

"I've got the music lined up. Most of the vendors. I wanted to end with a fireworks display for the grand finale, but I'm a little short on funding. I know the auction at the actual festival goes to the next year's festival, so I'm guessing not a lot was raised at last year's festival."

Beverly walked up, balancing their plates

and catching the last of their conversation. "Did I hear you say you're short on funding?"

"Some. There are a few more things I'd like to do, but I'm a firm believer in staying within budget." She gave a resigned sigh. "Especially fireworks. I remember that from when I was a girl."

"We haven't had the fireworks in years. I miss them. Let's make that budget larger." Beverly's eyes lit up. "I could have a small display of things for sale to raise money for this year's festival. There's room over by the lending library. We'd just have to get some donations. I could donate some baked goods."

"I'll donate some tickets to the play opening at the theater," Tori chimed in. "I always love the fireworks at the end of the festival."

Maxine walked up. "You guys talking about the auction at the festival?"

"Actually, we need more funding for *this* year's festival."

"Oh, I finished that small table. How about I donate it for this year's funding and the desk can go to the auction for next year," Maxine offered.

"That would be great. I really appreciate this. Every little bit helps. And I'm trying to get more donations for the auction at this year's festival so next year you won't be so tight on funding." Amanda took out her notebook and scribbled across the page.

"If we can find someone to run the festival next year." Beverly poured Amanda more coffee. "We couldn't have pulled this year off without you."

"I'm just glad to help."

"And I'm sure Dale will donate something. I'll talk to him." Maxine paused. "Maybe something with a bit of history to it. That always seems to be a big draw."

Amanda turned the pages of her notebook and frowned. "That's another thing I don't have nailed down. I mean, it's called the Heritage Festival. And I don't have much... *heritage* for it. Historical things, I mean."

"We usually have a small display of things at the gazebo. Dale helps with that. He's kind of our history buff," Beverly explained. "And you know what else we could display? We've found some interesting and mysterious items recently. We've been trying to figure out more about them."

"Oh, what have you found?"

"A rolled up canvas that I found hidden in

the bookcase of my office. A painting of a building that looks like the one we used to have here by the landing, only not exactly like it."

"Then I found a letter hidden in an old purse. But the letter seems to be written in some kind of code." Maxine shrugged. "We couldn't really figure it out.

"And I found this beautiful pendant hidden in a drawer of the theater. We found out later it's Miss Eleanor's great-aunt's, but we don't know why it was hidden in the drawer." Tori shrugged. "Just another bit of town mystery."

"So we could put these with the heritage display. See if anyone has any more information about any of them." Beverly laughed softly. "Well, we're pretty sure Miss Eleanor knows something about the painting and the letter, but she's not saying anything. We'd love to know more about them."

"This will be perfect. We'll make a display and put up a sign asking if anyone has any information about the items." Her mind raced with ideas of how best to display the items. "I'm really glad I came in this morning. And for all the help you've all given me."

"No, we're thankful you took over the task of getting the festival all organized. Otherwise,

I'm afraid it would have just disappeared." A sad smile slipped across Beverly's face. "Another part of our town's history forgotten."

"I'm hoping I can make this festival one the town will never forget. Like I've never forgotten the festival I went to here when I was a young girl."

"I remember going to the festival when I was young, too." Tori's eyes lit up with the memories. "My grandmother and I always looked forward to it. I can't wait to go to it again."

Amanda felt the weight of responsibility to make the festival come back to its former glory. And hadn't that been the one thing she wanted to escape? All the responsibilities? But somehow, planning this festival was different. It was fun. And no one was constantly emailing her or texting her. She felt a sense of camaraderie with these women, and the chance to create something special for this town made it feel more like a labor of love than a burden.

All in all, a pretty nice escape from the reality of her life back in New York. Beverly and Maxine went back to work, their cheerful banter with the customers providing a cozy background. Tori regaled her with stories of her life on Broadway, her eyes lighting up as she talked about the plays and the actors she'd met, but she was most proud of all she'd done with the Magnolia Key theater.

All in all, a perfect and unexpected morning. Full of friendship and laughter that made her feel like she belonged.

CHAPTER 10

Connor was certain that Brooklyn had tied her shoe ten times this morning, insisting that he watch her each and every time. Not that he really minded. The kid's enthusiasm was catching, and he found himself smiling at her infectious energy.

Megan came out of the back bedroom, wiping the sleep from her eyes. "Wow, you let me sleep in. Thanks." She stifled a yawn, her voice thick with sleepiness.

"I got up quiet as a mouse, Momma. Didn't I, Uncle Connor?"

"Yep, you did." He'd been up early enjoying a cup of coffee when she came racing out to see him, full of energy.

"Why are mice quiet?" Brooklyn's forehead crinkled.

"Not sure, Princess. Probably so people won't know they're there." How did she come up with all these questions?

Megan walked over to the coffeepot and poured herself a cup, leaning against the counter. "So, what are the plans for today? You know, after I get some coffee in me and feel a bit more human."

"I want breakfast." Brooklyn set her hands on her hips. "I think I'm gonna starve if I don't get food soon."

He considered her request, glancing around the kitchen. "I've got some cereal in the pantry. Or toast?" He wasn't exactly sure what he had. He'd planned to go shopping with Megan today to buy all the kid-friendly food needed for their weekend stay. He wasn't exactly certain what Brooklyn liked to eat these days. Seemed like it was always changing. He'd stocked up on strawberries for their last visit—her favorite, he was certain—and she refused to even take a bite of them.

"Let's go out to eat breakfast like big people do."

"I could make pancakes," Megan offered,

peeking into the fridge. "Except that Uncle Connor doesn't have any eggs."

"Hey, I thought we'd go grocery shop this morning. Get things Brooklyn likes. And I don't have pancake mix either."

"No strawberries," Brooklyn insisted.

"Right, got that, kiddo."

"We could go out to breakfast. That's a good idea. Then we'll go to the market afterward." Megan took her last sip of her coffee and then set the cup in the sink.

"Or we could go to the market and then come back here and cook breakfast." He tried to counter them both, already sensing a losing battle.

"I'd starve by then." Brooklyn frowned at him, shaking her head, her curls bouncing wildly.

"Okay, okay." He raised his hands in mock surrender. "Out for breakfast, it is." He could never refuse a thing his niece asked for.

Megan grinned, amusement flickering in her eyes. "No use fighting it, is there?"

"We're going to walk though." He hoped that might use up some of Brooklyn's endless energy.

"I like walking." Brooklyn bobbed her head.

"We can walk everywhere here. It's fun. Not like at home where we have to get in Momma's car to go anywhere."

They headed out into the sunshine and crossed over to the boardwalk, the fresh sea breeze tousling Brooklyn's curls this way and that. She skipped ahead, then turned and raced back toward them. "Let's eat there." She flung out her arm, pointing to a nearby building. "The one with the coffee cup sign. Momma needs her coffee. She always tells me that."

"Is it a good place for breakfast?" Megan tilted her head, questioning him.

"Never been," he said flatly.

"Really? It's not like there are many places to choose from here on the island."

"I don't eat out."

Megan rolled her eyes. "Of course, you don't. You might—you know—see a person or two or something."

He glared at her. "I'm perfectly fine eating at home. I prefer it."

"You gotta get out more, brother dear. See what's happening around you."

"Yep, Momma says you spend too much time in your workshop and not enough out in the world." Brooklyn skipped again, twirled, and turned around. "Did you know the world was round?"

"I've heard that," he chuckled.

"Round like a ball. I have a ball at home that's red. Red is my favorite color."

Megan grinned at him. "How'd you like to face that energy every morning?"

"You're actually a lucky woman, Megs."

"I know I am." She nodded. "But I don't mind sharing her energy with you for a few days."

He opened the door to Coastal Coffee and Brooklyn skipped inside. He and Megan followed her in. Then he froze, feeling the air sucked out of him. There, sitting right in the front by a big picture window, was Amanda. The light streamed in, casting a warm glow on her shoulder-length brown hair. Her skin had a bit of tan now, not the pale color like when she'd first arrived on the island.

And why was he noticing all this now, anyway?

"Look, Momma. Miss Amanda is here." She raced over to Amanda's table. "Miss Amanda, hi, remember me? Brooklyn. I'm staying next door with Uncle Connor."

Amanda's brown eyes locked with his.

Brown eyes tinged with specks of honey? How had he not noticed before this? Her cheeks flushed as she turned her gaze from him.

Amanda widened her eyes in shock. As far as she knew, Connor never came to Coastal Coffee. She pulled her attention from Connor to Brooklyn. "Hey, there. Of course, I remember you. So you guys came for breakfast, too, huh?"

Connor and Megan came over to her table. "Morning, Amanda," Megan greeted her with a warm smile. "I see you had the same idea as we did. Breakfast out."

She put down her notebook where she'd been scribbling notes since Tori left.

"It was wonderful. I'd suggest the blueberry muffins. Or the pecan waffles are always good."

"I want waffles without pecans," Brooklyn insisted.

Connor remained silent. Fine. She didn't care.

"Hope we're not interrupting your work." Megan nodded toward the notebook.

"Just making some notes about the festival.

We're running a bit short of funding and Beverly—she's the owner of the cafe—offered to set up a small fundraising area here. We're looking for donations."

Megan touched Connor's arm. "Hey, you should donate one of your wood carvings."

He shot her a glare. "No, I don't think so."

"But—"

He cut her off with a brusque shake of his head.

Of course he wouldn't donate to help raise funds. He wanted nothing to do with her or the festival, or the town for that matter.

"I wanna go to a festival." Brooklyn danced from foot to foot. "Momma, can we?"

"When is it?" Megan asked.

"In a few weeks."

"We could probably come back for it." She turned to Connor. "If that's okay with you."

"I wasn't planning on going."

"Please, Uncle Connor. Please. Can we go? Please." Brooklyn looked up at her uncle with pleading eyes.

She saw the exact moment he crumbled against her relentless pleas. With a sigh, he ruffled Brooklyn's hair. "Of course we can,

Princess." But when he looked over Brooklyn at his sister, his expression showed a distinct lack of enthusiasm.

Megan ignored his look and turned to her. "Why don't you come over for dinner tonight? I'm going to make spaghetti."

"You are?" Connor's eyes lit up with surprise, but she wasn't sure if it was because his sister was cooking spaghetti or the fact that she'd asked her over for dinner.

"Yes, I am. And there will be plenty."

"Miss Amanda, come to dinner. Please, please, please." Now Brooklyn turned those pleading eyes on her.

She glanced at Connor's stony face but couldn't say no to Brooklyn just to please him. "Yes, I'll come. What can I bring?" She turned from Connor's glare to Megan.

"Nothing. Just yourself. About six?"

"I'll be there."

"Yay!" Brooklyn twirled around.

"Brookie, be careful." Megan stopped her daughter's spinning. "We should get a table. See you tonight."

"See you then."

The three of them walked toward an open table in the back. Brooklyn skipped through the tables as Megan tried to keep up with her. Connor trailed behind, his shoulders set. He slid onto his chair and gave her one last frosty glare.

Connor had a nice sister and a cute niece, but the man himself was impossible.

CHAPTER 11

Amanda got ready to go over to Connor's, still questioning her decision but knowing she never could have refused Brooklyn's pleas. Connor would just have to get over himself. And she liked his sister. She was so friendly and nice. Quite the opposite of her surly brother.

She selected a bottle of pinot noir to bring with her. Gathering her courage—which was silly because she was just going to a neighbor's house for dinner—she crossed the distance to Connor's cottage.

She knocked on the door and Brooklyn tugged it open and threw herself into a hug. "You came. Yay. We're gonna have the best dinner ever. And Momma makes the best spaghetti too. You'll love it."

Brooklyn grabbed her hand and tugged her inside, dragging her into the kitchen. Megan stood at the stove, stirring the sauce. The enticing aroma of onions, garlic, and a hint of oregano filtered through the cottage.

"You made it. Great." Megan flashed her a smile.

Connor lounged against the counter, a noncommittal expression on his face.

"I brought some red wine." She held up the bottle.

"Oh, that was thoughtful. Connor, will you open it and pour us some?"

He scowled as he took the bottle from her and turned away. But not before she heard him mutter under his breath. "More of a beer drinker, myself."

Megan shot her brother a pointed glare, but he ignored it and busied himself with the task of opening the wine. Amanda shifted self-consciously as the tension in the room clung to all of them like a soaked blanket.

"I set the table," Brooklyn piped up, cutting through the awkwardness. "And Uncle Connor doesn't have placemats like we have at home.

He should have some, shouldn't he?" The girl looked up expectantly.

"Uh…" Amanda hesitated. How should she answer that? Connor was already plainly displeased with her presence. She couldn't imagine critiquing his table settings on top of that.

"I told Momma we should get some for him for his birthday," Brooklyn continued, oblivious to the undercurrents in the room.

"That would be a nice gift." She glanced over at Connor, but his back was to her.

He finally turned around and handed a glass of wine to Megan and one to her. He pulled his hand back so quickly when he handed it to her that she almost dropped the glass. He strode over to the fridge, pulled out a beer, and popped the top. Then he lounged back against the counter, taking a long swig as if to prove his point.

She stifled a sigh. It looked like she could do nothing to please this man. She took a sip of the wine but its rich, vibrant flavors did little to soothe the knots in her stomach. She had half-hoped that coming here for dinner would break down the wall to Connor's gruff exterior. But as each moment crept by, the wall between them grew higher and more impenetrable.

"Amanda, why don't you take a seat? I just have to drain the spaghetti noodles and take up the sauce. And Connor, will you grab the salad out of the fridge?" Megan's cheerful voice forced its way through the brittle friction in the room.

Grateful for the distraction, she took a seat as Megan served up dinner. Connor sat directly across from her, his expression a careful mask of neutral indifference.

"So, how is the festival coming along?" Megan asked after everyone filled their plates.

"Pretty well. I have most of the things nailed down. Still need to get more for the art show." She deliberately didn't look at Connor when she said that. "And if the fundraiser at Beverly's raises enough, I'm hoping to have a fireworks display as the grand finale of the festival."

"Fireworks. I love fireworks." Brooklyn bounced in her chair, almost spilling her milk. Megan steadied the glass.

"I do too. There were fireworks when I went to the festival a long time ago. I was just a few years older than you are. I'd love to bring them back and recreate the magic for a new generation."

"If Uncle Connor gives you one of his carvings, I bet it would sell for a million dollars. Then we could have fireworks." She bounced in her chair again.

"Uh…" Connor had a deer-in-the-headlights look as he scrambled to turn down Brooklyn's request.

"Uncle Connor, you'll do that, won't you? We want fireworks at the end of the festival, don't we? And Momma will let me stay up late and watch them, won't you, Momma?" Brooklyn turned those pleading eyes on Connor.

Megan smothered a smile as she looked over at Connor, then turned to Brooklyn. "Yes, fireworks would be wonderful, honey. I agree."

"So, you will give her one, right?" Brooklyn pinned Connor with a non-wavering look.

Connor let out a long, resigned sigh. "Yes, I'll donate a carving. I don't think it will bring in quite a million dollars though, Princess." A faint smile tugged at the corners of his mouth.

"It will, you'll see." Brooklyn jumped and gave him a hug.

He wrapped his arms around her and still

couldn't quite hide his smile. Brooklyn sat back down. "It's gonna be the bestest festival ever."

Watching Connor interact with his niece gave Amanda a tiny hope that the man would one day soften. Maybe. Or maybe it was just her who rubbed him the wrong way.

They finished their meals with Connor mostly remaining silent save for the occasional yes or no answer if he was asked something directly. She couldn't help but notice the annoyed glares Megan was throwing toward her brother.

As they stood, Amanda offered to help with the dishes. "No, I'll get them," Connor insisted, taking her plate from her hands.

She wasn't sure if he was being helpful or just wanted her to leave. "Okay, then I guess I'll be going. I have a busy day tomorrow getting the fundraiser set up."

"I'm glad you came, Miss Amanda." Brooklyn hugged her tightly.

"I had a really nice time." She hugged her back, basking in the little girl's enthusiasm and affection.

"Brookie, time to go get ready for bed."

"Do I have to?"

"Yes." Megan gave her daughter a no-nonsense look.

"Ooooo-kaaaay." Brooklyn's shoulders slumped as she trudged from the kitchen toward the bedroom.

"Connor, you should walk Amanda back to her cottage."

"Oh, no. I'm fine." She looked quickly over at Connor. He looked relieved at her words.

Megan walked her to the door. "Thanks for coming. And I can't wait to come back for the festival. Brooklyn is so excited. It's really wonderful all you're doing for the town and the festival."

"Part of it is selfish. I want to recreate the festival that I remember from all those years ago."

Megan smiled. "And I have no doubt you will."

Connor methodically scrubbed each plate, the rhythmic motion a soothing balm for his chaotic thoughts. He carefully placed each item in the dishwasher. The faint sound of bedtime stories being read filtered down the hallway.

Megan returned to the kitchen and sank wearily onto a chair. "I read her three books, and she still wanted more. I think she's just wound up from all the excitement of being here. And she can't quit talking about the festival. I hope it's okay if we come back for it."

"Of course it is. You know I love having you two here." He started the dishwasher, and it hummed to life before he crossed over to sit across from his sister. He could tell by the look on Megan's face she had something on her mind. And he was pretty sure he didn't want to hear it. Distracting her seemed like a better option. "Your spaghetti really is the best, you know."

"You want to talk about food. I want to talk about… Amanda."

"Why?" His voice was sharper than he intended.

"Because I like her. And I'm glad you gave in to Brookie's pleading and offered to donate one of your carvings. I hate how you keep all of your beautiful art tucked away in your workshop."

"Can we not discuss this, Megs?"

"Not discuss Amanda or not discuss your art?"

"Both. Let's not discuss either one."

Megan leaned forward, ignoring his remark. "I think it's great that Amanda is jumping in to help make sure the festival happens this year."

"I thought we weren't talking about Amanda."

"No, *you* thought we weren't talking about you. *I'm* talking about her. You should be friendlier toward her."

"I'm friendly," he muttered, almost to himself.

Megan laughed. "As if. And you barely said a word during dinner."

"The three of you had enough words for everyone."

His gruff, defensive manner didn't fool her. She reached out and gently touched his arm. "Connor, I don't know why you act like this. All gruff and grumpy. Because you're really not like that. You're kind and generous. Or you used to be before you decided to become this reclusive artist."

He sighed. So much for not talking about his art, either. "I just like my solitude, Megs. Like to work alone. And... well, I'm pretty much done with showing my artwork. I can't believe I gave in to Brooklyn. Those eyes of hers. Who can say no to them? And I felt like if I said no, I would be personally responsible if she didn't get to see her fireworks."

"You would have been." Megan's lips twitched as she tried to hide her smile.

"I just hope they raise enough, or it all will be for nothing."

Megan's eyes softened, and she squeezed his hand. "You know, Connor, someday you're going to have to get over it and put it behind you."

He looked at her for a long moment, hesitating before answering. "I have no idea what you're talking about." But, of course, he did. But they sure weren't going to talk about *that*. Not now. Not ever.

CHAPTER 12

Amanda wrestled with the folding table, huffing in frustration as she tried to get it set up where Beverly had made space for her. But no matter what she did, the fourth leg stubbornly refused to open. Her cheeks flushed with exertion and annoyance, and she just barely restrained herself from kicking the exasperating thing. She didn't know if she was annoyed more at the table itself or at Connor for the way he'd acted so dismissively and cold toward her last night. The man had an uncanny ability to infuriate her.

Stepping back, she took a deep breath and then turned her attention back to the table, determined to conquer the thing one way or another.

She looked up in surprise to see Connor standing before her, hands causally tucked into the pockets of his well-worn shorts, watching her. "Need help?"

Before she could answer, he reached down and flicked the lever—the very same one she'd been messing with for over five minutes—with a deft movement. With a smooth pull, the last leg opened obediently. He flipped the table over and set it in place effortlessly.

"How'd you do that? I've been working on it forever," she blurted out, unable to hide her exasperation.

"I pushed the lever?" he answered matter-of-factly.

"I did too. But it wouldn't open for me." She stepped back and crossed her arms defensively. "Anyway, thanks for the help," she added, not wanting to sound ungrateful.

Then he reached behind him and retrieved a carving from a table near them. "Here."

He thrust it into her hands. She caught her breath as she examined it carefully, turning it this way and that. Two doves sat on a curved magnolia branch. Their feathers were meticulously carved with intricate detail. A delicate magnolia blossom adorned the branch, its petals unfurling with lifelike grace. "Connor, it's beautiful." Her fingers traced the smooth contours of the wood.

He shrugged again, his expression nonchalant. "Just a little something for the fundraiser since I promised Brooklyn."

"Well, thank you. This will really help."

"I doubt it helps much." He dismissed her gratitude with a wave of his hand.

She frowned for a moment, studying his guarded expression. "You don't take compliments very well, do you?"

"I—what?" He scowled, obviously caught off guard by her observation.

"You should be proud of your work. It's wonderful."

"I am proud of it." His jaw tightened ever so slightly.

"Then why don't you show it?" she challenged, her gaze holding his.

He ignored her question. "If that's all you need, I'll be leaving. Taking Brooklyn for a swim."

He strode out of the cafe, and she stood there holding the carving, marveling at its delicate curves and the beautiful tones on the wood. He was amazingly talented. And all that talent was hidden in his workshop. It didn't seem right. But then, it wasn't her decision to make, was it?

Connor eased himself down onto his worn couch cushions and put his feet up on the coffee table. The old wood table creaked under the weight. He truly enjoyed it when his sister and Brooklyn came to visit him. He did. But Brooklyn was a whirlwind of activity—though he adored her—and his sister asked entirely too many questions. He settled back on the couch and took a moment to savor the stillness broken only by the steady ticking of an old antique clock hanging on the wall.

The peace was short-lived when an insistent knock sounded at the door. He reluctantly pushed up off the couch, annoyed to have his solitude interrupted again so soon. Who needed his attention now?

He crossed to the door and flung it open. His eyes widened in surprise to see Amanda standing there.

"Hi, Connor. I brought over slices of peach pie for the three of you for your dessert tonight. Just a thank you for Megan inviting me over last night. I'm still learning how to bake pies. I hope it's good." She held out a plate.

"Uh… they just left."

Disappointment crept over her face. "Oh, I'm sorry I missed them."

The rich aroma of the freshly baked pie wafted toward him, enticing him. And he swore he felt his sister nudging him. Chiding him. Her voice rattled in his brain, insisting he ask Amanda in. *Be nice to her.* "Would you like to come in? We could, uh… each have a piece of pie?"

Amanda's eyes widened slightly and a flicker of surprise crossed her face at his unexpected offer. Well, fine. He was startled by the words that had tumbled from his lips too. Why on earth had he invited her in?

A warm chuckle reverberated through the room as if Megan was offering an approving *"Good Man."* Now he was imagining things.

"Um… sure. I could come in." She gave him a tentative smile.

He stepped back to let her pass, then closed the door behind her. He took the plate from her, its sweet contents enticing him as she followed him into the kitchen. He got out two plates and placed the pie on them, then dug in the silverware drawer for forks. He handed her a plate.

"Thank you."

"Here, take a seat." He cleared off a stack of Brooklyn's books from the table.

Amanda took a seat, and he sat across from her. He took a bite of the pie and tasted its sweet and tangy flavor. He didn't bake pies and rarely ate out, so this was a nice treat. "This is really good."

She blushed at the compliment. "Thank you. I keep trying to improve the crust."

"Not sure you could improve on this crust."

Her eyes lit up in pleasure, then she ducked her head, concentrating on her pie. They sat in silence for a bit, eating. She finally broke the silence. "I do appreciate you donating for the festival fundraising."

He nodded. Then he swore his sister kicked him under the table. "You're welcome. Hope it helps."

"I really want to be able to have the fireworks." She set her jaw in a determined line.

"Everything going okay with the planning?"

The words seemed foreign as they left his lips. Chitchat. He was making an effort, just like Megan requested.

"It is. But I'm afraid I'm not going to get everything finished in time. I only had a few weeks to plan all this. Usually, I plan out my events way in advance."

Another phantom nudge from Megan, and he had to look at the empty seat to make sure his sister wasn't sitting there. "So you need help?"

She looked at him skeptically, one eyebrow arched. "Are you offering?"

He hesitated for a moment and took a deep breath. "I guess I am." What? Was he crazy? Did he really want to do this?

Amanda's skepticism was replaced with a glimmer of hope in her eyes. "Do you have time tomorrow to go through pieces for the art show? I need to figure out a way to display them all. We're going to have the show at the large pavilion at the park. And we'll save an area for some of the historical items to be displayed too."

"I could do that." A sense of begrudging resolve settled over him.

"They're all at my cottage."

"I'll come over in the morning and we'll look through them." His offer lent a hint of purpose that he didn't even know he'd been lacking.

No, his life was fine the way it was now.

"Thank you. I really appreciate it. I'm sure I'll need some easels for paintings and I'm not sure what all else."

"We'll figure it out." We? We? How did he get involved in this whole festival thing? He could only blame his sister's phantom pokes and her words echoing in his mind, urging him to open up and quit being such a recluse.

Amanda finished her piece of pie and stood up. "I don't want to keep you. But thanks for asking me to join you. I'm glad you liked the pie."

"Pretty great, if you ask me." He stood, his chair scraping lightly against the wooden floor. He collected their plates and set them in the sink with a soft clatter. As he escorted her to the door, the gentle scent of jasmine wafted in. A familiar scent that seemed to follow in Amanda's wake.

"I'll see you tomorrow. Thanks for offering to help." She slipped out the door, giving him a parting smile.

A smile that stirred something deep inside him, long hidden. But he ignored it as he softly closed the door, already warring with his decision to help. Hadn't he told her repeatedly he liked his solitude?

And did he want to get involved with anything dealing with the art world again? No, he didn't. He knew that answer deep in his soul with unwavering certainty.

But he'd help her this one time, a reluctant concession to Megan's nagging. And he'd tell Megan about it too. That should give her—and him—a temporary reprieve.

Yet, even as he agreed to help this one time, he braced himself for the inevitable onslaught of encouragement that would accompany Megan with her impending return in a few short weeks. Her determination to coax him out of his shell and prod him into sharing his art with the world would undoubtedly resurface when she returned.

He knew his sister was just worried about him. She cared about him, he knew that. But sometimes she pushed him a bit too much.

He picked up the stack of Brooklyn's books and put them back in the guest bedroom. He couldn't believe the amount of books and toys he'd accumulated over the years for her visits. And that didn't even count the ones he sent home with her. Oh well. What's an uncle for if not to spoil his niece?

CHAPTER 13

The next morning, Amanda was up early, sorting through various items for the upcoming art show at the Heritage Festival. Paintings, sculptures, and other local artworks were scattered across her living room, waiting to be organized. She hummed softly to herself as she examined each piece, trying to envision the perfect arrangement. A knock at the door interrupted her thoughts, and she went to the door, half surprised that Connor had kept his promise to help her.

"Come in."

He stepped inside and swept his eyes around the room, taking in her organized chaos.

"There is kind of a method to my madness. At least I thought there was." She looked at the items placed on the table and set on the couch. "Or… maybe not."

He crossed over to the table and picked up a hand-thrown pottery vase, examining it closely. "This is nice work." His voice carried a tone of genuine appreciation.

"I think it's pretty." She picked up a framed picture. "And this is an original illustration from Heather Parker. She's local to Moonbeam Bay. A lot of her work is printed commercially on t-shirts and mugs and things like that."

Connor scowled and turned around but not before she would swear he muttered, "That's unfortunate."

He picked up a hand-sewn quilt, tracing a finger along its even stitches. Then he sorted through a stack of framed photographs of different landmarks on the island.

"That's from a local photographer. She does good work, doesn't she?" she asked, trying to gauge his reaction.

"She has a fairly good eye," he admitted, though his tone suggested reluctance.

He picked up a sea glass necklace and held it to the light.

"That's a local too. She makes all sorts of items from sea glass."

"Looks like it's just that cheap broken glass you can order online anywhere. Not sure it's really sea glass."

"Well, it's really pretty, whatever she uses." She defended the necklace because it was beautiful.

He grunted and turned to a hand-knit lace shawl. He didn't say a word about it and continued looking through the items. No words of praise. Nothing.

Connor turned to her, his blue eyes reflecting a mixture of reluctance and curiosity. "All right, let's see what we can do."

For the next hour, they worked together, sorting and arranging the items into thematic groupings. Connor offered suggestions on how to best showcase certain pieces, his knowledge of art and design becoming increasingly apparent as he engaged in the task.

As they worked together, he seemed to warm up to the job at hand, his attitude softening as he admired a hand-blown glass ornament that perfectly captured the colors of the sea. He picked up a set of hand-dipped candles. "Lavender. And a mild scent, not too overwhelming like so many candles."

He looked around at their piles, neatly

sorted now. "I think you're going to need some walls to display some of this. The pavilion is open air."

"I'm not sure what to do about that." She frowned, considering their options and the logistics.

"I could make you a few display walls. Use pegboard and then you can use hooks to hang the items."

"You'd do that?" she asked, surprised at his offer.

"Yes. And don't worry. I'll make the bases sturdy so they won't blow over if we have a windy day."

"That would be so helpful." She looked at him closely, genuinely stunned he'd offered to help even more. She liked this new Connor a lot more than the gruff, standoffish one.

Connor shook his head, surprised he'd offered to help yet again. But it wouldn't take him long to make the display walls for her. A quick trip to the hardware store for some pegboard and hooks, and he'd be set. Besides, he was beginning to grudgingly admire her commitment to making the town's festival a success. And the way her eyes lit up when she picked up a piece of the artwork, appreciating the skill that was poured into the work—it stirred something inside him. It was hard to resist her infectious enthusiasm and nearly impossible not to get roped into her plans.

"So, do you think you would change your mind and display a few of your carvings in the art show?" Her eyes were hopeful, pleading. So similar to Brooklyn's when she wanted something from him.

The question caught him off guard and hung in the air between them. Of course, this was the price he paid for offering more of his help. Now she wanted his art.

"I don't really do art showings anymore."

"Why not?"

"Got my reasons." The words came out blunter than he intended.

A look of hurt settled on her face before she struggled to compose herself. "Okay. Just thought I'd ask again."

He let out a long, weary sigh as he swore he felt his sister jab him in the side. "Okay, maybe just one carving."

Amanda's eyes filled with excitement.

"Really? Oh, Connor. That's wonderful. Thank you."

For a moment he froze, sure she was going to launch herself into a hug, just like Brooklyn when she got her way. Luckily, Amanda stopped just short of that but did grab his hand.

He stared down at their hands, her small hand smooth against his calloused one. How long did they just stand there? He pulled his hand back and cleared his throat. "We could go over to the workshop now and pick out which one you want." He paused and looked at her sternly. "But I get the final say. No arguments."

"Yes, that's fine."

With the soft crunch of sand beneath their feet, they made their way over to his workshop. He threw the doors open wide and let the light spill into his studio. He had designed the workshop with care, strategically placing windows on all sides to let in the most natural light possible. His workshop was his most favorite place on earth. His sanctuary. The one place he was truly at peace.

He turned around to see Amanda standing tentatively in the doorway. He motioned to her, the corners of his mouth tilting up ever so slightly. "You can come in, you know."

She nodded and stepped inside, looking appreciatively at his artwork. He restlessly stepped from foot to foot as she wandered around the shop, looking at each carving. "I can't choose. You should." She came back to stand in front of him, her face a mixture of appreciation and indecision.

"Okay, I'll choose." But why was he so nervous?

He walked over and picked up a carving of a seagull, its wings stretched out in mid-flight. He carved the details of its wings with painstaking precision. The carved bird was held up by a curved piece of wood that he'd reworked over and over to get the braided look just like he imagined it.

He crossed the room to another shelf and picked up a carved sea captain outfitted in a rain slicker and hat. The sea captain held a pipe in one hand and a bucket in the other. The carving capturing the essence of a life at sea.

He returned to Amanda. "How about one of these?"

She looked at them closely. "I love them both. Each in its own way." Her voice was full of admiration.

117

He sighed, a small smile creeping over his lips. "Okay, you can have them both."

She clapped her hands in delight. "Really?"

He nodded and set them on his workbench, the carved seagull and sea captain resting among the array of tools and wood shavings. She wandered over to a life-sized carving of a blue heron, its slender body captured mid-stride. "This is so beautiful."

"That's carved out of cherry. I loved the colors of that piece of wood, and the lighter sapwood accentuates the details of the feathers."

She touched the wood lightly, stroking it. "It's the most magnificent piece of work I've ever seen."

Her sincere praise pleased him, even though he thought he was way past what anyone thought about his work. But he did care what she thought. Her appreciation awakened something long buried.

He cleared his throat as emotions he hadn't expected swept through him. "That was the first piece I carved after I moved here. I wasn't sure I was ever going to carve again when I first came here." He touched the wood, smooth from hours of rubbing oil into it. "I busied myself building this workshop and… one thing led to another. Seeing the herons wading along the shore, watching me, their graceful swoops as they take off—it reignited the spark of creativity I'd been missing."

"I'm glad you didn't stop carving. These are all so lovely. I know you said not to ask... but why not show them? Share them with the world?"

Her honey-brown eyes held that pleading look that he couldn't resist. Asking him to open up, to explain. But he wasn't ready for that. "I do have my reasons," he said softly. "Things happened that made me disillusioned with the art world. Things I couldn't change, but things I didn't want to be a part of any longer. So I left that all behind me. Left New York City. Moved here."

"You're from New York, too?"

"I am, and I don't miss it a bit." Okay, he did occasionally when he let himself remember the good times there. The excitement of a big art show opening. The thrill of seeing his art at prestigious galleries. When an art critic would praise his work. The satisfaction when a buyer's eyes lit up when they found a piece of his art that spoke to them and they just had to have it.

But then... all that changed with one

mistake. A mistake born out of naivety and misplaced trust. But he couldn't go back and change it any more than he could fix the consequences.

Amanda was oblivious to the turmoil rolling through his memories. She smiled and said, "It took me a bit to get used to the slower pace here. But I enjoy it now. It will be hard to go back."

"You're going back to the city?" He tilted his head, studying her expression.

"Yes, this is just a sabbatical. I needed a break from… everything. The calls, the texts, the emails. The… rush."

"And you took on running the festival? Isn't that counterintuitive to your need to step back?" He couldn't stop the hint of amusement in his voice.

She smiled softly. "I guess it is. But I've really enjoyed working on the festival. And you know what? Magnolia Key people are not constant texters like New Yorkers. I like that. I like being here." She shrugged. "I didn't know what to expect when I came here, but I seem to have gotten more than I bargained for. I love it here."

"I think you're doing a fine job with the

festival. You seem very organized. You've done a lot in the short time you've had."

She sighed, a flicker of uncertainty crossing her eyes. "Now if I can just finish up everything in time. And get the townspeople won over a bit so they aren't so skeptical I can pull this off."

"You will. And I'm going to help you." He didn't know what came over him, but he had this strong desire to help this woman. Make sure her festival turned out exactly how she'd planned it. Show all the townsfolk what she was capable of.

As if on cue, Megan's voice echoed in his mind in a tone of sisterly pride. "*Way to go, baby brother. Way to go.*"

But he silently reminded himself to be careful. Not to be so trusting. Because he vividly remembered what happened the last time he blindly trusted someone.

CHAPTER 14

A manda got up early, as usual. Her days were busy with tasks for the festival, but each night she indulged herself in reading before bed. A new habit that she promised herself she wasn't going to give up when she returned to New York. She was totally engrossed in another book she'd picked up from Beverly's lending library. It was nice to turn off the electronics and just enjoy a good book in the evenings.

Unexpectedly, Connor had become an invaluable help the last few days. Offering to go to the mainland to pick up supplies. Calling vendors. And, of course, making the display walls for the art show. She didn't know how she would have gotten all this accomplished without him.

And just as surprising, she found herself thoroughly enjoying his company. He even occasionally smiled now. And just last night he'd had a glass of wine with her while they went over the plans.

She headed into Coastal Coffee this morning to grab a quick breakfast and see how the fundraiser was going. She stepped inside to the now familiar and welcoming embrace of the aroma of freshly brewed coffee and yeasty pastries.

Beverly greeted her and waved. Amanda headed over to the fundraising table, scanning the array of donated items. She noticed that Connor's carving was no longer on the table.

"Beverly, where's Connor's carving?" Amanda asked as Beverly came over.

"It sold. I was just getting ready to call you. And you won't believe how much it sold for. The guy said he refused to be outbid and put down this offer." Beverly pulled out a piece of paper from her pocket. "The guy was adamant. He looked at the carving carefully and turned it over. Then insisted he wanted to buy it no matter the cost. Even if we don't make much from the rest of the donations, you'll for sure have enough for the fireworks."

Her jaw dropped at the number. "Oh, wow. This is wonderful news. Fireworks." A broad grin spread across her face. "I'm so excited. I need to call the fireworks company. They know what I want and were just waiting for my final go-ahead."

Her heart swelled with gratitude for Connor's donation as well as the mysterious benefactor who had recognized the true artistry and value of Connor's work. Now she could forge ahead and make the festival all that she'd dreamed of.

"You here for breakfast too?" Beverly nudged her.

"I am. I'll just grab a table."

Beverly came over and poured her coffee, then set the pot on the table. "The usual?"

"Yes, please. I can't get enough of the pecan waffles."

Beverly nodded. "And I see that Connor has been helping you with the festival. And rumor has it he's putting a piece of his art in the art show."

"He's putting two pieces in it. I was surprised he agreed to it."

"You two have been seen together all over town." Her eyes twinkled with friendly curiosity. "Is there something going on between you? More than just festival work?"

Heat rose in her cheeks at Beverly's suggestion. "No, of course not. He's just being helpful. He's a nice guy. And… I guess my first impression of him was wrong."

"He sure didn't do much for the town before you showed up," Beverly said, a hint of amusement in her tone. She grinned as she headed off toward the kitchen to put in the order.

Just then Miss Eleanor walked into the cafe. Amanda waved, and Eleanor bobbed her head slightly in acknowledgment before making her way over to the table.

"I just got back in town. How are things going with the festival?" Miss Eleanor asked, all business, no pleasantries.

"They're going great. I'm wrapping up loose ends. And we did a small fundraiser and raised enough funds to end the festival with fireworks like you used to."

"You did?" Miss Eleanor's eyes widened with surprise before she nodded in approval. "I knew we made the right decision to bring you on board with the planning. We needed someone with experience to get us back on track. I hope you're keeping notes of all you're doing. Whoever takes over next year will surely appreciate having the notes for a reference."

"I will write up some notes. That's a good idea."

"And the art show?"

"I've got plenty of local art ready for the show. And we're going to have a small display of some historic items at the show too."

"That's a good idea."

"It was Beverly's."

"What was mine?" Beverly asked as she walked over and set down a plate of pecan waffles on the table.

"Your idea about displaying the history items at the art show."

Beverly's gaze flicked quickly to Miss Eleanor, then back at her. "Yes, a few antiques that Dale has come up with from his shop. And did Amanda tell you we're going to have fireworks? Won't that be a delightful treat? Just like we used to have."

She would swear that Beverly was changing the topic from the historical items. Maybe she just didn't want to take credit for the idea?

"She told me. And it will be nice to have them again. It's been years. I used to so enjoy them." Eleanor nodded. "I'll just grab my table now. You'll bring my coffee?"

"Yes, of course." Beverly nodded. "I'll grab your cream."

"And you let me know if any problems come up." Eleanor pinned her with a stern look. "We can't have any problems, can we?"

Amanda understood the message. The success of the festival was of utmost importance. She couldn't really say that the planning so far had been without *any* problems. But, as always, she'd do her best to fix any future problems that arose.

Amanda finished the last bites of her waffles, savoring the nutty flavor of the toasted pecans and sweet maple syrup. She said goodbye to Miss Eleanor and Beverly before heading back outside. She blinked against the brightness, Beverly's words echoing in her mind. Something going on between her and Connor. Of course not. He was just a friend. He was a friend, right? More than just an acquaintance? Okay, she wasn't sure where their relationship stood, but she was grateful for his help. That's all it was.

She pushed her tumbling thoughts aside. It

was a beautiful day. The sun warmed her skin and the light breeze tousled her hair. Perfect weather. She just hoped the weather held out for the festival too. Right now, predictions were okay, but it was too far out to be certain. Storms had a way of popping up unexpectedly on the island.

But all in all, she was very pleased with how everything was going so far. As she walked down the sidewalk, the owner of a small shop stopped her and offered up some Magnolia Key t-shirts for the auction for next year's funds. Another townsperson converted and trusting her. She smiled as she continued down the sidewalk, pleased with herself and the progress she'd made.

The president of the bank said hello and called her by name. She was finally starting to get known around town.

Yes, everything was working out perfectly.

CHAPTER 15

Late that afternoon, Amanda took a long beach walk, enjoying the gentle coastal breeze as it tossed pieces of her hair that escaped her French braid. The waves lapped gently over her feet, inviting her to pause and savor their soothing rhythm. She breathed in the fresh, salty air and relished the sense of relaxation that flowed through her. A feeling that just a few short weeks ago would have been totally foreign to her but now wrapped around her with familiarity. She finally turned around and headed home, surprised that her cottage did feel like home for her here on Magnolia Key.

As she neared her cottage, she saw the doors were wide open to Connor's workshop. Intrigued, she paused, observing him from a distance. He sat inside working, his head bowed over his workbench, deep in concentration. She wasn't sure if she should disturb him. She knew he was adamant about his solitude when he worked.

Right then he glanced up, his eyes meeting hers. He waved and motioned for her to come. She crossed the distance and stood in the doorway. "I don't want to bother you."

"You're not."

"But you're working." She nodded at the piece of wood on the table before him.

"I am…" He paused for a moment, a slight hint of uncertainty crossing his features. "But I wouldn't mind some company." He motioned to a stool beside the workbench.

His unexpected offer caught her off guard. "I can… watch you work?"

He nodded. "Sure." He gestured once more to the vacant stool.

The man was full of surprises. She went and perched quietly on the stool near his workbench. He turned back to the wood, and she watched his hands work, fascinated by their skilled movements. She sat there in silence, mesmerized as the wood began to take shape under his talented hands. The corners of his eyes crinkled with his concentration.

Time seemed to slow, the world outside fading into the background. The intimacy of the moment tugged her into its embrace. The golden light filtering into the workshop. The sounds of his tools scraping the wood. It was just the two of them existing in their own little world.

"Oh, it's a pelican." The words slipped out. Amanda worried that he didn't want her chattering while he worked, disrupting his creative process.

To her surprise, he look up and smiled at her. Did he know his smile was becoming almost commonplace? Where was the gruff woodworker she'd met when she first came to the island?

"It is a pelican. Or will be. Been working on it a few days." His eyes lit up with passion as he talked about his work.

"I think it's magical the way you can create something so incredible from just a piece of wood. And then it becomes something… beautiful. It comes alive."

He looked at her closely, as if truly seeing her for the first time. "Thank you," he said softly, his voice filled with appreciation for her understanding and recognition of his art.

The golden light spilled into the workshop, illuminating the moment, as the two of them shared this intimate appreciation for the transformative power of creativity and craftsmanship.

"I think it must be so wonderful to create something like that. Take something raw and transform it into something beautiful and real."

"Do you paint or draw or do any kind of art?" He tilted his head, his eyes filled with curiosity.

"No. Not really. I never had time to try my hand at anything." A wistful smile played at her lips.

"Maybe you should. You never know what hidden talents you might have."

"Maybe I will." Not that she had any inkling of what she might try or where to even begin.

With a soft groan, he stood up and rolled his shoulders. "I should probably quit for the day. Losing the light too."

Disappointment tugged at her. The moment was broken. "Oh, I should go." She could have sat there for hours watching him work and being sucked into his world.

"I—" His forehead crinkled. "Actually... would you like to come in and have a drink? I don't have any wine like I know you prefer. Just beer."

"Beer sounds perfect." She said the words almost too quickly. His offer was yet another surprise, and she was happy to have a drink with him and prolong their time together. Although he probably just wanted to talk about the festival plans.

"Good. Let's go." He closed the workshop doors, and they headed up on his porch, the boards creaking softly under their steps. "Just take a seat. Be right out with the drinks."

He returned quickly and handed her a bottle of icy cold beer. "Thanks."

"Oh, did you want a glass? Where are my manners?"

"No, the bottle is fine."

He sank onto the chair next to her and stretched out his long, tanned legs. A faint dusting of sawdust clung to this shirt, and he absentmindedly swiped at it before taking a swig of his beer.

She took a sip of hers, enjoying the rich, amber liquid as it slid down her throat. "This is so good."

"This is a local craft beer I pick up when I'm over in Moonbeam Bay. Have you been there? Or over to Belle Island? There's this little cafe right on the beach that I went to once. Magic Cafe. Great food. Have you explored around the area much?"

"No, just here on the island." Her gaze drifted out to the expanse of beach before them and the swaying fronds on the palm trees. "And I'm not sure I feel like I've seen everything the island has to offer yet. I am planning on going to a play. I'm anxious to see what Tori has done with the theater."

"I've heard a new show is opening. Maybe we should both go."

"You mean together?" she blurted out in surprise.

A low chuckle rumbled from Connor's chest. "Yes. Unless you'd prefer to see it alone."

Heat crept across her cheeks as she stumbled on her response. "No. I mean yes. I mean, sure, let's go together." She nervously tucked a loose strand of hair behind her ear.

"I could pick up the tickets. Saturday work for you?" he asked casually, as if the whole thing wasn't any kind of big deal.

She nodded, still stunned at his offer and not

sure exactly what the offer was. Was he thinking it was a date? Had he asked her out? Or was it simply friends heading to a play together?

"Connor, you know what?"

"What?" He stopped mid-sip and looked at her over the top of his beer.

"You're different than I expected."

"Different how?"

"Well…" She considered her words carefully, "You were kind of… gruff when I first met you."

"Megan would say I was rude." He laughed. "I've just been on my own for a while now. Working alone. I'm not much of a people person. It's just… I do like my solitude." He shrugged, downplaying the admission.

"Yet you asked me to join you in your workshop tonight. Watch you work."

He stared at her for a long moment, his forehead wrinkling. "Because… you don't feel like people. You feel like… a… friend. And you're easy to be with. Nice to talk to." His voice was low as if he were revealing something deeply personal. Then he quickly shrugged, as if dismissing his thoughts. "I just felt like having you there with me."

Her heart fluttered at his unexpected

candor. "And I was thrilled to be there. Watching you work was… moving, Connor. Really. You are so talented."

He held up a hand, a self-deprecating chuckle escaping his lips. "Okay, but can we come to an agreement?"

"Sure."

"You won't nag me to show my art like Megan does." A hint of pleading flickered across his features, revealing a touch of vulnerability that contrasted with his rugged exterior.

She snapped her fingers. "That reminds me. The piece you donated. The doves? It sold. It sold for enough to cover the fireworks."

His eyes widened, then narrowed. "It did? Who bought it?"

She detected a hint of wariness in his tone. "I don't know. Beverly said someone came in and saw it. Asked if it was a Connor Dempsey piece of work. Examined it closely. She said they even turned it over to look at the bottom of it. Then he wrote a big check and left."

He frowned. "He looked at the bottom of it?"

"Yes. Why?"

A muscle twitched in his jaw. "I carve a

symbol on the bottom of my work. Kind of my personal signature. The symbol is one I found in my grandmother's old sketchbook."

"So someone who knew of your work would know you do that?"

"I do it now on all my more recent carvings. But my older pieces, from when I was first starting out…"

A bit of a disgruntled look crept over his rugged features. And she'd swear a hint of anger flashed in his eyes before he let out a long sigh.

"You okay?"

"Yep, I'm fine." The corner of his mouth quirked up in a wry grin. "Just thinking about the follies of youth. The mistakes we make when we don't know better."

She was thoroughly confused by his cryptic answer but didn't want to press him. He'd opened up to her, and she didn't want to break the moment.

They sat on his deck, watching the breathtaking display as the setting sun painted the sky in magnificent streaks of orange and yellow. The colors danced and wove together, creating a mesmerizing view that stretched across the horizon.

She finally broke the comfortable silence

and turned the conversation to Megan and Brooklyn, asking questions about them. He regaled her with stories of Brooklyn's antics, and his love for his niece shone clearly in his eyes.

As the evening wore on, she finally looked at her watch. "Oh, it's getting late. I should probably go," she said reluctantly, not wanting the moment to end but knowing it was time to go.

Connor stood, his tall frame unfolding gracefully. "Here, I'll walk you home."

She stood up beside him and wondered where was the man who'd refused his sister's request that he walk her home after their spaghetti dinner? He still had his hard edges. He still had an air of mystery about him. But there was a softer side to this man that hinted at a depth of character and a capacity for kindness that she felt herself drawn to.

They descended the steps together, their footsteps muffled by the soft sand beneath their feet. As they crossed the beach in the gathering darkness, he took her elbow, a touch that was both reassuring and electrifying.

They climbed the steps to her porch. Suddenly, the moon popped out from behind the clouds and threw silvery rays of light around them. He stood there in front of her. Just stood there. His eyes locked on hers with an intensity that made her heart skip a beat.

She held her breath. A flutter of anticipation stirred in her chest.

"Good night, Amanda," he said, his voice barely above a whisper. Then with a slight nod, he turned and went down the steps before jogging across to his cottage.

Left alone in the moonlight, she gazed up at the stars. A question hung in the air as real as the breeze caressing her skin. Had Connor Dempsey been on the verge of kissing her?

And an even more intriguing question—had she wanted him to kiss her? The attraction between them was undeniable. At least, she thought it was. Maybe. As she slipped inside her cottage, the questions lingered, promising to occupy her thoughts long into the night.

Connor, buddy. What have you done?

Connor trudged up the steps to his cottage, retrieved their empty bottles, and walked inside. He put the bottles in the recycling, the sound of glass on glass breaking the silence of the cottage.

He rinsed out his coffee cup from this morning and put it in the dishwasher. His stomach rumbled, reminding him that he really should eat.

But instead, he found himself drawn back outside. The worn boards were smooth under his bare feet. The gentle breeze played with his hair. The stars stretched above him in a dance of constellations. All of it was so familiar—and yet so different.

Had he truly asked Amanda out on a date? The question hung in the air, twisting and spinning like the mobile he'd made for Brooklyn when she was a baby.

Did she think that's what he'd done? Well, he kind of did, didn't he?

She was just so effortless to be around. And he admired so many things about her. The way she organized this festival and didn't seem to let anything ruffle her feathers. The way she seemed to enjoy Brooklyn's boundless energy. The way she'd looked at him tonight…

And he'd felt an intimate connection with her when she sat there silently watching him work. He never allowed anyone to watch him work, guarding his solitude carefully. But tonight he'd glanced up a few times, seeing her eyes light up with recognition and appreciation of the craftsmanship of his work. And he'd been delighted when she realized he was carving a pelican with her keen observation and admiration.

He shoved his hand through his hair, looking out at the moonlight glistening on the waves, his mind in turmoil, surging like the tides.

Yes, Connor Dempsey. What have you done? What have you set in motion with this lowering of your carefully constructed walls of protection?

CHAPTER 16

The next morning Amanda woke up in a great mood, humming softly while she made coffee. She took the steaming mug outside onto her deck. Not because she was hoping to catch a glimpse of Connor or anything. It wasn't that.

Everything was going so well right now. The festival planning was going smoothly. She and Connor were getting closer, and she liked that. And she had a date—or was it a not-date—with Connor to go to the new play at the theater. A smile crept across her lips as she stood and sipped on the coffee, running memories of last night over and over in her mind. Watching him work. Their time sitting on the deck.

Okay, she really needed to work, not sit here

and think about Connor all day. She returned inside and flipped open her laptop. An email from one of the festival sponsors caught her eye. She clicked on it and a heavy feeling hit the pit of her stomach. They were pulling out due to what they said was a significant downturn in their business and they weren't certain sponsoring the festival was a good business decision now.

Before she could fully process the ramifications of that, her phone buzzed and she opened the text from the funnel cake vendor. They were having problems with their equipment and had to cancel too.

She was almost afraid to answer her phone when it rang, but she did, only to be informed that one of the singers in the barbershop quartet lost his voice and they were hoping to find a replacement for him

Amanda regretted her naive, positive mindset of this morning, thinking everything was going as planned…

The weight of these setbacks clung to her, but as much as she needed to solve these problems, her thoughts kept drifting back to Connor. Not a very productive way to handle things.

Disillusioned by the morning's setbacks, she headed to Coastal Coffee, hoping Beverly might have a lead on another sponsor.

She headed inside and sat at the counter, watching as Beverly efficiently waited on another customer, then she turned to her. "What's up? You look a little frazzled."

"A sponsor pulled out."

"Luckily your fundraising sales are going like gangbusters here. I've had so many people come in and donate things. And everything is selling. I think the town is starting to really get excited about the festival this year. Everyone is talking about having fireworks again."

She blinked, surprised at Beverly's words. "Wow, I thought that everyone was still doubting me. Not trusting an outsider to plan it all."

"You're winning them over."

Amanda grinned despite of all the problems of the morning, her spirits rising at the growing enthusiasm of the town. "Well, that's good to hear. Now I need a new funnel cake vendor because I just have to have funnel cakes. I remember them from when I was young."

"Let me make some calls with some of my

suppliers. Maybe someone will have a connection."

"Thank you, that would be great." She sighed. "Now if the baritone in the barbershop quartet could just get his voice back or they find someone to fill in for him…"

"Bet it all works out," Beverly said encouragingly, her optimism infectious.

"I hope so."

"Pecan waffle?"

"I think I'll just have the yogurt and granola. And more coffee, please."

"You sure?" Beverly's eyebrows arched, a playful challenge in her voice.

"I'm sure." She couldn't eat pecan waffles every day of her life, could she? Besides, she'd put on some weight since she'd arrived here in Magnolia. Not surprising since she skipped so many meals back in New York, just not taking time to eat.

Beverly brought her food out and slipped behind the counter. She waved to a woman coming in and the woman walked over to them. "Darlene, have you met Amanda?"

"No, but I've heard about her and all she's doing for the festival. Nice to meet you,

Amanda." Darlene reached out and shook her hand.

"Darlene owns the Bayside B&B," Beverly explained.

"Nice to meet you, Darlene."

Darlene sat down beside her. "Just coffee. Thought I'd pop in on my way to the market."

Beverly brought her a mug and turned to Amanda.

"So what else is new? Connor still helping you out?" Beverly said as she took out a stack of napkins and silverware.

"He is. And yesterday he invited me into his workshop to watch him work."

"You don't say." Beverly mindlessly made up a napkin roll, her hands moving with practiced ease. "That's surprising."

"It was. And it was fascinating. I could have sat there for hours watching him. Then we had a drink."

"Sounds like he's opening up a bit to you."

"He is. Some," she said noncommittally. "I find it so intriguing that he can create something so beautiful out of nothing. Well, out of a block of wood. I bet that's a great feeling. He asked me if I had tried any artistic endeavors, but I had to admit I hadn't."

"How about trying your hand at knitting?" Darlene asked. "I'm always hoping to convert people into knitters. I have my knitting group. We love newcomers. I could teach you to knit. That's creating something out of nothing. Okay, yarn in this case."

She considered the offer. "I think I'd like to try knitting." The idea of learning a new skill appealed to her.

"Great. We're meeting on Monday. About ten at the B&B. I'll have yarn and needles for you. I have way too much yarn. More than I can knit in my lifetime." Darlene laughed and shrugged her shoulders, her expression a mix of amusement and self-awareness. "But it's what knitters do when we're not knitting. We collect yarn. I've got needles too. You'll be all set. We'll start you out on a simple scarf."

"Thank you. I can't wait."

"You're making all kinds of new friends here, aren't you?" Beverly smiled. "Like Darlene and Connor."

"I guess Connor and I are friends. And…" She looked at Beverly for a moment before blurting out, "And we're going to the play at Tori's theater on Saturday." She positively ignored the flutter of excitement that swept through her. She did.

Beverly's hand paused mid-air. "Together? On a date? I'm pretty sure Connor has never been on a date since he moved here."

"I'm not sure if he thinks of it as a date or not. Maybe just friends going out to a show?"

Beverly smiled. "Maybe."

She dug into her yogurt and tried to ignore the fact that it wasn't a pecan waffle. She comforted herself by saying it was definitely healthier for her.

Tori came into the cafe and up to the counter. "Morning all." She slid onto the stool next to her. "You'll never believe who came in and bought two tickets to Saturday's show."

"Connor Dempsey?" Beverly asked and grinned.

"Wait. How did you guess?"

"Because one of those tickets is for Amanda." Darlene laughed, her eyes twinkling.

Amanda's cheeks grew warm. "We're... ah... going together. I'm honestly not sure if it's a date though."

"Going to a show together sounds like a date to me," Tori said as she took the cup of coffee

Beverly handed her. "So, you two are getting close?"

"Close? No, we're just friends. I think. I mean we're closer than when I first came to town and he wanted nothing to do with me. But under all that gruff exterior and his claiming he needs his solitude... there's a really nice guy."

Beverly looked at Tori and Darlene, a knowing glance passing between the three of them. "Bet there's something going on there."

"Sounds like it." Tori nodded.

"Hey, I'm sitting right here. How about we just wait and see how Saturday goes before jumping to any conclusions?" She shook her head. "I mean, maybe we're just friends?" Were they? Is that all they were? How come this was so confusing?

"Well, we can't wait to talk to you after Saturday night." Beverly headed over to wait on a customer.

Amanda hoped that after Saturday, she'd have a better idea of what her and Connor's relationship actually was. She frowned. And what did she want it to be? The honest truth was she did like him, maybe more than she cared to admit. She liked him a lot. But he was here, and she lived in New York, so maybe they shouldn't even start anything. That would be the reasonable choice. And she was always reasonable, wasn't she?

CHAPTER 17

On Saturday, Amanda opened the door to Connor's knock. The sweet scent of magnolia floated in from the tree near her front porch. He was dressed in khaki slacks and a knit shirt that hugged his frame just right—clearly, clothing he'd slipped into without fuss. However, she was kind of proud of herself for only changing her outfit once while getting ready. Okay, twice.

"You look very pretty." His glance swept over her.

Heat rushed to her cheeks. "Thank you."

"Are you ready?" he asked, a hint of nervousness in his voice.

"I am. We're walking, right?" She struggled

to keep her tone light and casual in spite of the butterflies in her stomach.

"If that's okay with you."

She nodded as she stepped out on the front porch. They set off down the street. As they strolled along, friendly faces greeted her by name now, their smiles and waves a sharp contrast to the anonymity of her daily life in New York. She was getting used to it and actually enjoyed it. She'd miss it when she went back home. Although the thought of New York and living there seemed like a distant memory for her now as she'd become accustomed to her life here.

"Evening, Amanda, Connor." Beverly waved from across the street, breaking Amanda's thoughts of New York. "Have fun."

She waved back. "Hey, Beverly." A warm feeling of belonging swept over her, an unfamiliar feeling that she hadn't experienced in far too long. Or perhaps it was more, something she'd been searching for without even realizing it. She had to remind herself this was only temporary. But in that moment, she was glad she offered to help with the festival because this way she got to meet so many people on the island and they were starting to get to know her.

As they reached the theater, Tori was standing out front, welcoming patrons. The former Broadway star looked radiant with her now-gray hair swept up in an elegant bun with tendrils framing her face and her eyes sparkling with enthusiasm. Amanda admired the woman's ageless beauty and poise.

Tori took Amanda's hand as they approached. "I'm so glad you two could make it. I hope you'll like this production. We have some very talented actors and they've worked so hard."

"I'm sure we'll love it."

Connor gave their tickets to the attendant and they headed inside to find their seats. She looked up at the magnificent, sparkling chandelier above them. The beautifully restored interior looked just like she remembered from when she'd come to a play with her parents. Tori had put so much care into bringing the historic building back to its former glory. "It looks great, doesn't it?" she whispered to Connor as they walked down the aisle.

"It really does."

They slipped past a few people already seated in their row and settled into their seats, Connor's arm brushing hers slightly as they sat down. She stole a glance at his strong profile as he bent over, reading his program. Despite her initial reservations about their date, not-date, excitement fluttered through her.

The lights dimmed and the lush red curtains swept open with a flourish. A hush came over the crowd as the first actor came out on stage. She leaned back in her seat and soon was lost in the story unfolding onstage but still acutely aware of Connor being right beside her.

She was so engrossed in the play she was surprised when intermission seemed to arrive so quickly. "Do you want something? Food or a drink?" Connor asked.

"I'm fine."

"You look like you're enjoying the play." He smiled at her. A smile she was beginning to get used to seeing on his features.

"I am. I know I'm used to seeing plays on Broadway, but Tori has really outdone herself with this production. It's wonderful and worthy of a run on Broadway. The actors are great and the staging is breathtaking."

"I kind of regret not coming to the theater before this. A whole new experience for me. I'm really enjoying myself," he admitted with a bit of surprise in his voice.

Soon the lights flickered, signaling the end of intermission. A hush came over the audience again as the play resumed. She was instantly lost in the storyline again, captivated by the performance. Her heart raced as the final curtain fell, and she joined the audience as they rose to their feet and thunderous applause echoed in the theater. As they made their way outside, Connor led her over to Tori who was standing by the doors, talking to people as they left.

She hugged Tori. "It was wonderful. You must be so proud."

Tori returned her hug, her eyes sparkling with joy. "They did a wonderful job, didn't they?" She passed the compliment off onto the actors.

Gratitude for her friendship with the woman crept through her. She'd met so many warm and welcoming people here on Magnolia. Stepping back, she added, "And the theater is beautiful. You did a wonderful job restoring it."

Tori beamed. "Thank you. I think she turned out beautifully. A perfect place to perform our plays and share the magic of theater with the community."

Other patrons grabbed Tori's attention, and

Amanda and Connor headed down the street, back toward their cottages. The balmy night was laced with the tangy scent of the ocean and the sweet fragrance of flowers in bloom. The streetlights cast a warm glow around them as they slowly strolled along the sidewalk.

She still didn't know if they'd had a date or not, but she'd thoroughly enjoyed herself. She was just sorry the night was coming to an end. "Thank you for suggesting we go together to see the play. I had a wonderful time."

"I did too."

She paused under a streetlamp and he halted beside her, looking at her questioningly. Gathering her courage, she voiced the uncertainty that had been lingering in her thoughts. "I just have to ask… did you consider it a… date?"

Connor's gaze held hers, his eyes intense yet unreadable. "Did… you?"

She blushed as she stumbled over her words. "I… think so?"

To her relief, his mouth tilted into a slight reassuring grin. "Good, because I did too."

He took her elbow, and they continued walking. So now her question was answered. It was a date.

As they neared her cottage, he turned to her. "Would you care to come over for a drink? Or is it getting too late?"

"I'd love to." Anything to prolong this wonderful evening.

She settled comfortably on a chair on his deck as contentment settled over her. He soon returned with a bottle of red wine, a small platter of cheese and crackers, and a plate of sliced apples. "I hope this is okay. I don't know much about wine. Had to ask a guy in the wine section of the grocery store."

His humble admission was endearing. "It looks great. That's one of my favorite wineries." She nodded toward the label and relief shone on his face.

"Oh, good." He poured them wine and sat on the chair next to her. The night air wrapped around them like a soft blanket, and the gentle sound of the waves splashing against the shore was a soothing soundtrack.

For a few blissful moments, they sat in silence, the stars poking through the velvety darkness above them. He finally broke the stillness. "So, Amanda Kingston, tell me about yourself. I know you're a big-shot event planner in New York. What else? Family?"

She took a deep breath, tracing the rim of her glass with one finger before setting it on the small table between them. "Not any close family," she began, trying to make her voice sound steady. "My parents died when I was young."

"I'm so sorry."

"I thought maybe Megan told you. We talked about it when she was here."

"She didn't say a word. Probably thought it was your story to tell."

She fought back the pangs of pain that still dug at her when she thought about that time of her life. "We had just vacationed here on Magnolia Key. It was such a magical trip and I have such great memories of it. Only a few weeks later, they were killed in a car accident."

She paused, and he nodded at her encouragingly. "Go on," he said softly.

"Then my grandmother took me in. She was wonderful. She helped me adjust to… to everything. But then, she started having memory problems. At first, it was just not remembering a word here or there. Then one day she forgot how to make toast. She laughed about it, but from then on I tried to do everything I could for her."

"That must have been really tough."

She glanced up at the stars before continuing. "It was. Eventually, she was diagnosed with Alzheimer's. I tried to hide the fact she had it from everyone, but the family found out and decided I couldn't live with her anymore. That she wasn't fit to take care of me. I moved around between different family members until college, and from then on, I lived on my own. I still went to visit her as often as I could. I tried to see her every week. She eventually had no idea who I was, and it broke my heart. Not only because I missed the woman she was, but she was lost in this world where she just didn't know where she was, who she was, who anyone was. It's such a horrible, horrible disease."

He reached out and squeezed her hand. "I'm sorry that happened to her. To you. But she was lucky to have you for a granddaughter."

A lone tear trailed down her cheek. "I… I miss her." She dashed at the tear and cleared her throat. "And my parents, of course. But I lived with Nana for more years than I lived with my parents. It's kind of strange to think of it that way."

"You've had some pretty deep losses." He still held her hand in his.

"Megan said you two lost your parents too."

"We did. But we had each other, so that helped."

"And Brooklyn's father?" The question slipped out before she could stop it, curiosity getting the best of her.

He frowned as a touch of anger flashed in his eyes. "He's... he's out of the picture. Left when Brooklyn was a baby."

"I think it's nice that you and Megan are so close."

"She and Brooklyn are my world," he said simply. "Adore them both."

She studied the man sitting next to her and wondered how different her life would have been if she'd had a sibling to lean on through all the losses. Someone to share the good and the bad times.

"So, is that why you came to Magnolia Key for your break?" he asked gently.

"It was. I had such great memories. I was a bit uncertain at first. Thought maybe it would be too hard to come back here. But I feel like I'm surrounded by good memories when I'm here. Like... like I'm still close to my parents."

She shrugged self-consciously. "That probably sounds silly."

"Not at all," he assured her, his thumb caressing the back of her hand, a simple, comforting gesture.

At that moment, she felt such a strong connection to him, one that went beyond the short time they'd known each other. It was as if the shared vulnerabilities and understanding had bonded them, drawing them closer.

She looked down at her hand still wrapped in his strong one as if he was giving her strength to tell her story. She reached for her glass with her other hand and took a sip. They sat there, hand in hand, as the gentle breeze caressed them. A lone gull called out as he soared past. This was a night she would remember for a long time. A perfect evening.

They finished their wine and snack and she reluctantly rose. "I should get home. It's really late."

He nodded and took her hand, his calloused fingers interlaced with hers as they crossed the cool sand to her cottage. They stood facing each other at the door. Tension crackled between them, and a look flickered across his face that she knew said he wanted to kiss her.

But he didn't. The moment lingered, then he simply reached up and swept a lock of her hair away from the side of her face and traced his thumb across her cheek. "Good night, Amanda. Thank you for a wonderful night," he murmured, his voice low and husky.

She swallowed hard against the lump forming in her throat. "Thank you. I… I had a great time." She barely managed to get the words out.

His lips curved into a brief smile, and he headed back to his cottage. She reached a trembling hand up to where he had touched her, feeling the lingering heat.

"I can't quite figure you out, Connor Dempsey," she said softly into the darkness.

CHAPTER 18

A manda didn't see one sign of Connor on Sunday, not that she was really looking for him, of course. Much. His workshop door remained closed, and she never saw him out on his deck. But that was okay, she told herself. She had lots to do for the festival.

She got up early on Monday and made a light breakfast before heading over to Darlene's for her first knitting lesson. She walked over, the morning sunlight illuminating her steps as she crossed over to the bay side of the island and found Darlene's bed-and-breakfast.

A cozy Victorian-style house sat back with a long lawn stretching before it. Wicker chairs were scattered across the front porch, inviting everyone to come and sit down. Cheerful flowerpots spilled over with bright blooms. She climbed the stairs a bit nervous, but excited.

"Come in," Darlene greeted her. "We're just getting started. Here, take a seat by me."

Amanda was acutely aware of the friendly but curious glances as she sat down beside Darlene.

"Ladies, this is Amanda. She's a brand-new knitter. And she's the one organizing the Heritage Festival this year."

The women greeted her warmly. Darlene introduced her to everyone, and each one showed her their project, from a lacy shawl to a striped baby blanket to a light cotton sweater. A Mrs. Thompson was busy knitting a baby sweater for her first grandchild in a delicate shade of pink. A younger woman, Sally Ann— *was that her name?*—was knitting a bright pair of socks. The pastor's wife was knitting a prayer shawl, her nimble fingers moving with ease and grace.

Watching their skilled hands, she felt a twinge of self-consciousness. She wasn't sure she'd ever get to their level of mastery, but at least she was going to give knitting a try, ready to start her new creative endeavor.

"Now, here are the needles I have for you. Some nice bamboo ones. They won't be as slippery as metal ones." Darlene handed her the needles and then plucked a skein of soft, creamy yarn from the basket in front of her. "And I have this worsted weight yarn. A good yarn to learn with—not too thick or too thin. First, I'm going to teach you an easy cast-on. That's where you start to put stitches on the needles."

She watched Darlene carefully as she demonstrated, her fingers deftly moving the yarn and making stitches magically appear on the needle. Then she tried it on her own as Darlene patiently corrected her and soon she had a row of stitches—albeit uneven ones—on the needle.

"That's enough for a simple scarf," Darlene nodded. "Now I'll show you the knit stitch."

She struggled a bit at first but soon got into more of a rhythm with the movements, and they didn't feel so strange. Her stitches weren't as even as Darlene's, but she kept trying, each row looking marginally better than the last. The friendly buzz of conversation and clicking needles surrounded her as she concentrated on her work. Darlene kept nodding encouragingly at her as her work grew slowly.

"I heard that we're going to have fireworks again this year at the festival." Mrs. Thompson's voice cut through her intense concentration.

Amanda paused, stilling her needles, though Mrs. Thompson seemed quite capable of knitting and speaking at the same time. "We are. We raised enough funds and I've got them all ordered."

"I'm pleased to have fireworks again. It's been years." Mrs. Thompson smiled approvingly. "You're doing a great job with the organization this year. I'm afraid the last few years we just couldn't get people to volunteer or donate. I'm willing to help with anything you need. Just ask."

"I'll help too," Sally Ann offered.

"Thank you, both of you." Soon the others were offering up items to be donated to the auction for next year's festival.

As they all turned back to their work, a sense of belonging crept through her. She looked around at the women, busy chatting and knitting, their needles never pausing. A sense of kinship surrounded the women, a camaraderie that was unfamiliar but something that she craved. Just simple friendship and a sharing of a craft they all enjoyed.

After a few hours, the group slowly disbanded, with everyone heading out. She looked at her slightly lopsided beginning of a scarf and was proud of what she'd accomplished.

"You take that with you," Darlene said. "And here's a bag I knit. You can use it to carry your project. If you have any problems, you just drop by here and I'll help you. And if you come next week, I'll show you how to purl."

"Thank you, Darlene. I really had a good time. You have such a nice group of friends."

Darlene smiled. "I do, don't I? I'm a lucky woman. And I'm glad you joined us. You're welcome anytime."

She headed outside with her knitting project carefully placed in the cute bag Darlene had given her. Hopefully she wouldn't forget all she'd learned by the time she got home. She'd love to keep going and get a few more inches done on the scarf this evening. But now, she needed to get back to wrapping up details for the festival.

When she got back to her cottage, she set her knitting out beside her favorite chair and went to her laptop to check emails. She clicked through them one by one, jotting notes to herself when needed.

She looked at the next email in surprise. She'd reached out to a friend in New York who'd given her the name of an art critic. Her friend heard the woman was doing an article on regional art shows. Amanda had written to the woman but hadn't heard back. It was a long shot, anyway.

But here she was, replying. The woman wanted to do a preliminary viewing of the items in the show. She wanted to do a write-up of the show but had a conflict on the actual date of the festival. Pleased, Amanda quickly answered back that it would work. An early write-up might help with promo for the festival too.

Luckily she had most of the artwork staged now in a large room in city hall, waiting to be moved to the pavilion for the festival. She wished she could set up the artwork at the pavilion for the critic, but it really needed to stay inside and protected until the festival. She'd have to make sure everything looked great and the lighting was good.

She finally rose and stretched, walking over to the sink to grab a glass of water. Glancing outside, she saw that Connor's workshop doors were open. She debated going over there but didn't like to interrupt his work uninvited.

She hadn't seen him since the almost-maybe kiss on Saturday. A flutter of insecurity swept through her. Maybe he was avoiding her? Maybe he hadn't had as good a time as she had? Or he was regretting his decision to go on a date with her?

She turned away from the window, determined not to go over. He could come see her. She didn't want to look like she was chasing after him…

She settled into the overstuffed chair and picked up her knitting. Soon she was engrossed in her project, the rhythm of the needles and the dance of the yarn feeling more and more familiar as she practiced.

A knock at her door startled her, and she put her knitting down. She walked over and opened the door, pleased and surprised to see Connor standing there. "Hey, you." A warm smile turned up the corners of his mouth and his eyes twinkled.

"Hi." Her breath caught.

"Wondered if you needed any help with anything for the festival. I've got some free time on my hands."

"I'm actually pretty well set. If the weather just holds out. That's one thing I can't control."

"It wouldn't dare rain on your parade." He winked at her.

Connor Dempsey winked. A smile slipped across her lips. "It better not."

"So if things are going well and you're not busy, you want to take a walk on the beach?"

"I'd love to." She kicked off her shoes, leaving them on the weathered porch steps as they stepped into the late afternoon sunshine.

They headed down to the beach, the powdery sand shifting beneath their feet until they hit the hard-packed sand by the water's edge.

"This never gets old," he said, nodding out toward the water. "The view of the waves, the clouds up in the sky, the birds flying past. It's like a living piece of artwork. When I lived in the city, I felt like all I got were brief, teasing glimpses of the sky."

"I know what you mean. Bits of sky between all the skyscrapers. Trees just in the few parks scattered around, all boxed in by concrete." She glanced out toward the horizon where the turquoise water met the blue of the sky, the vastness of it all almost overwhelming her. And the fact that she was here, right now, taking it all in, appreciating it.

"And I admit to liking the sound of the surf better than the honking of cars and the sounds of sirens." He watched the waves lap at his feet. "It was a good decision for me to move here. To... get away." He turned back to her and smiled. "Guess I'm just in a reminiscing mood today. How things were, how they are now."

"It seems like a different world than the one I came from. I'm really enjoying my time here." And she could barely admit to herself that she'd been thinking about extending her visit. She'd already scheduled two whole months off. What would be left of her business if she took even more time off?

He looked down and gently took her hand in his, his fingers intertwining with hers as if it was the most natural thing in the world. They turned and headed down the beach, their steps in sync as the wind gently swept past them. The waves raced up the beach in front of them and washed away their footsteps behind them.

Contentment settled over her at the rightness of her life these days. Life here on Magnolia, with the friends she'd met and with Connor, filled her with a joy she hadn't known she was missing. With a bone-deep sense of belonging. And with the certainty she was where she was supposed to be right now. She glanced up at him and he smiled back at her. If the man didn't watch out, his smiling might become a habit.

CHAPTER 19

Amanda's fingers trembled slightly as she arranged the items for the art show, wishing she could be doing this at the actual pavilion. There she could spread them out more artistically in the groupings Connor had come up with, to better highlight their artistry. But this cramped room in city hall would have to work for now.

The door swung open, and a woman strode into the room dressed in a flowing skirt and silk blouse, her steps confident as if she owned the room. Extending a perfectly manicured hand, she introduced herself, "Desiree Knight."

"Miss Knight, nice to meet you. I'm Amanda Kingston, the event coordinator."

"I was a bit surprised at how difficult it was

to get here. Needed to take the ferry. I see they are building a bridge. That will make the trip to the island much more manageable." Desiree swept her gaze around the room with a look of distaste. "This is where you're doing the show?"

"Oh, no." She rushed to explain with an apologetic smile. "We're having it at the big open-air pavilion. It will be the perfect place to display the artwork. This is just where I've been staging the show to keep the items protected. I'll set it all up at the pavilion when the festival begins."

"I see." She took a measured step forward, her heels clicking on the tile. She tilted her head, scrutinizing one of the paintings resting on an easel. "Ah, a Heather Parker illustration. Her art is simple and has a nostalgic tone to it."

Amanda couldn't tell if that was a compliment or a subtle critique. "So what paper did you say you were from?"

Desiree waved a dismissive hand. "I write for many papers. Freelance. This is for an article on small, regional art shows. Hoping to get a good placement for the article. I'm going this weekend to a festival in Naples. Quite a large one."

Sensing a hint of condescension, she raised

her chin. "Ours isn't that large, but we do have some excellent quality work."

"Hm," Desiree answered noncommittally.

The woman wandered around, looking at the items with a discerning eye. Her face was a mask of neutrality. A knot of nerves tightened in Amanda's stomach as the woman looked at each item and took a few notes in a sleek leather notebook, her expensive fountain pen scrawling across the page.

Desiree picked up Connor's woodcarving and turned it this way and that, frowning with perfectly arched eyebrows. She put it back down on the table and turned away without writing a note.

"That's lovely work, isn't it?" Amanda interrupted. "He's a local and very talented."

Desiree turned to her. "I suppose for local talent, all these items are reasonably well-crafted. To be quite honest, I'm not sure what I was expecting from these regional art shows. I'm used to doing reviews for some bigger showings in New York and Los Angeles. Also covered a large one in Taos. Those tend to attract artists from all over the country."

"Well, our Heritage Festival aims to

celebrate the island's rich history and focus on the incredible talent of our local artists."

"Yes, I can see how such a quaint idea would hold appeal for the local community." Desiree flipped her notebook closed with a decisive snap. "I do appreciate having the chance to prescreen the art since I'll be at another, larger show the weekend of your festival."

"I'm glad you could come and see the work of our talented artists." Amanda guided Desiree out of the room and to the front door of city hall.

Desiree glanced at her watch. "Oh good, if I hurry, I can catch this next ferry back to the mainland. Good luck with that bridge. I hope it gets finished soon for the sake of all of you stuck on the island."

Amanda watched the woman walk away and a sinking feeling began in the pit of her stomach. She wasn't sure she was going to like the article the woman wrote. She seemed singularly unimpressed with any piece of art and unable to see the heart and soul the artists had poured into each piece.

If it was merely a freelance piece, perhaps the woman wouldn't even secure an offer to publish the article. Amanda could only hope.

She headed down the sidewalk, her sensible flats scuffing against the concrete as she made her way back toward her cozy cottage.

She couldn't worry about the article now. She had things to do. And she didn't care if some stuffy city woman wasn't impressed with their festival. It was going to be a fabulous event, and all she wanted was for everyone to enjoy it. Especially all the townspeople who had finally come around to accepting her and appreciating her hard work organizing everything.

CHAPTER 20

A few nights later, Connor asked her over to dinner at his place, and there was no doubt this time he considered it a date. He blatantly stated it was. Excitement and nervousness fluttered through her as she slipped on a simple sundress, the soft cotton fabric caressing her skin. She carefully curled her hair, leaving it down to drift around her shoulders in soft waves. A touch of mascara and a light sweep of coral lipstick added a touch of color to her face. If she was ready, then why was her heart beating faster? She dug in the drawer, found some blush, and swept a brush of it across her cheeks, giving them a healthy glow. With one last look in the mirror, she turned and headed to the door.

She stepped out onto her deck and saw Connor out lighting the grill on his porch. He saw her and waved, a smile spreading across his features. She raised her hand in a slight wave, her silver bracelets jingling, and crossed the sandy expanse between their cottages. She climbed up his wooden stairs and dropped her shoes onto the worn planks, slipping them on quickly.

He crossed over, took her hand, and squeezed it. "Glad you could come over. I'm grilling some grouper. Hope that's okay."

"Sounds absolutely delicious." She loved being on the island and the easy availability of a variety of fresh fish.

"Made a salad and a potato casserole recipe my sister gave me. If it doesn't turn out, we'll blame her." He chuckled, his eyes crinkling at the corners. "But I picked up some pie slices from Beverly. Didn't trust myself making dessert."

"I'm sure it will all be wonderful."

"Why don't you make yourself comfortable? I'll go get us some wine."

"You know you don't have to drink wine just because I like it. You can drink your beer," she offered, not wanting him to feel obligated.

"What can I say? I've developed a taste for it myself these days. I got help picking out this bottle too. Hope you like it. It's a pinot grigio. Supposed to go well with fish." He headed inside and she stood at the railing for a moment, watching the waves. Something so soothing and comforting about their endless movements.

She turned when she heard him come back out, the soft creak of the deck boards announcing his return. He handed her a glass and clinked his lightly against hers. "To hoping the meal turns out." He grinned widely.

"To a nice evening." She took a sip and savored the crisp, tangy flavor. He'd once again picked out a perfect wine.

"Come, keep me company while I grill the fish. Won't take long. Everything else is ready."

She followed him over to the far end of the deck and leaned against the railing, watching his movements as he placed the fish on the grill and sprinkled an aromatic seasoning over them. He concentrated on his grilling while she watched. He soon flipped the fish over. He looked up and caught her watching him. "Doesn't take long for it to cook."

She'd never grilled fish, so she didn't know the particulars, but it smelled delicious. He took up the fish on a waiting platter and they headed inside, his free hand resting on the small of her back in an effortless, familiar gesture.

They walked into the kitchen and she saw that he'd set the table and placed a small vase of flowers in the center. He laughed. "Still don't have those placemats and cloth napkins that Brooklyn was complaining about. But knowing my sister, I'll have them the next time they visit."

"It looks lovely," she assured him. She slipped into a chair as he dished up the meal and sat down across from her. The meal was delicious. The fish was delicately seasoned to perfection, the salad crisp with a tangy dressing, and the potato casserole perfectly done and piping hot with a crispy layer of crumb topping. "This is all so good."

"Thanks. I'm not the world's best cook, but I do cook a lot. Much prefer it to going out to eat."

"I eat out all the time in New York. Or grab take-out. I've been experimenting with recipes and doing lots of cooking since I got here and have more time. I'm really enjoying myself."

"I'm usually a meat and potatoes kind of guy. Usually baked potatoes or sometimes I dice them up and fry them."

"My grandmother taught me how to make potato pancakes from leftover mashed potatoes. Really yummy."

"I don't think I've ever had them."

"I'll have to make them for you." And just like that, she'd almost invited him to dinner. She paused, then continued. "Would you like to come for dinner tomorrow night?"

He grinned at her. "If we keep this up, we'll be having every dinner together."

"We might." That idea didn't bother her a bit.

"I'll be there."

After they finished their meal, they cleared the table, but he insisted he'd do the dishes later. They headed back outside to enjoy the sunset. He lit candles in the lanterns lining the deck, and they cast a magical light in dancing patterns on the worn planks.

"Here, let's sit on the glider." He motioned to the loveseat-sized glider fashioned to look like a double-sized Adirondack chair.

They sat down, side-by-side, and he gently pushed them, setting the glider into a gentle swaying motion. "This is nice," she said. "And it's really comfortable."

"Thanks. I made it. I think it's Brooklyn's favorite place to sit."

"So you do woodworking besides just carvings?"

"Some. Made a baby cradle for Brooklyn and a toy chest. Oh, and a rocking horse."

"You've got quite a lot of talents with wood then, don't you?"

"I do like working with it. Finding the perfect piece of wood. The grains in different types of wood. How it takes stains."

"Well, it's not the same, but I learned to knit this week." She laughed. "Darlene taught me, but I'm not very proficient at it. She's going to work with me some more next week."

"My mom was a knitter. She loved it. I swear she could look at any knitted item and make it herself—with improvements. I still have an afghan she knitted me and a hat. And a sweater that no longer fits, but I can't seem to give it away." He shrugged. "Maybe Brooklyn will wear it one day."

"I'm sure she'd love that. The connection with her grandmother."

"I'm sorry Mom wasn't around to get to meet Brooklyn. She would have loved being a grandmother."

"I bet she would have."

"I know it's been years, but I still miss her." His eyes were lined with pain, maybe softened over the years, but pain still lingered. He took her hand, their fingers intertwining. "But then, you know what I'm talking about."

"I do. I miss my mom, my dad, and my grandmother. I guess especially Nana. It was just the two of us for so many years. We were so close. Maybe even brought closer by her Alzheimer's disease. Fighting it together. Adapting to life as she declined. I just wish… I wish I could have helped her more. Stayed with her longer."

"I'm sure she appreciated all you did for her."

They sat in silence for a while, each one lost in their memories. She finally rose. "I should go. It's getting late."

He stood beside her. "Is it wrong to say I don't want you to leave?" A hint of vulnerability laced his words.

"I…" What was he asking? Her mind scrambled as she tried to decipher his question.

"I mean, I like spending time with you. It always seems to go by so quickly."

"It does." She nodded, thankful he wasn't

asking her to spend the night. Because she wasn't ready for that. Not that kind of intimacy. Their connection still felt fragile.

He took her hand and led her back to her cottage. He stood facing her, holding her hands. "Would it be okay…" He paused, looking deep into her eyes. "Would it be okay if I kissed you?"

She nodded silently. He lowered his lips to hers, the lightest brush like the flutter of butterfly wings, then pulled away slightly. His intense gaze locked with hers. He dipped his head again and kissed her deeply, a sigh escaping his lips. When he finally pulled away, he wrapped his arms around her, holding her close to his chest.

Her heart ricocheted, racing a race that had no end. She could feel his heart thrumming against her cheek. After several long moments that still weren't long enough, he loosened his embrace and stepped back. He brushed his thumb along her jaw. "Good night, Amanda."

"Night," she answered, wondering if he could even hear her words as they drifted off into the night, carried away on the ocean breeze.

CHAPTER 21

Amanda couldn't get Connor's kiss out of her mind. Not while she made coffee the next morning. Not while she worked on her to-do list for the festival. Eventually, she surrendered to the persistent thoughts and decided to channel her energy into dinner preparations. She did a quick run to the grocery store to get what she needed to cook for Connor tonight. She'd go ahead and make the mashed potatoes early so she could then fry up the potato pancakes. Rosemary chicken and asparagus would round out the meal. She also bought apples to bake a pie.

She hurried home to get started. Connor's praise for her peach pie crust came to mind as she mixed the dough and rolled it out. She couldn't resist adding a touch of artistic flair with a fancy design on the top crust and a cute edging that she had seen while browsing the internet.

She set the table and used some pretty placemats that the owner of her rental had provided. They made her smile, thinking that Brooklyn would like that she had them.

After feeling like she had things under control, she sat down at her computer to work for a bit. She flipped open the top and navigated her inbox, clicking through the emails. She had web alerts set up for Magnolia Key Heritage Festival, and she clicked on an alert to see who had mentioned them.

It was a post on social media. She clicked over to it and started reading. Her breath caught as she scrolled. Desiree had indeed not been impressed with the artwork for the festival and hadn't minced words. Her heart sank when she read the scathing words the art critic had used to describe Connor's work. Trite. Similar to a mass-market carving she'd recently seen but admittedly with a nicer piece of wood. Desiree went on to say she hoped the other regional art shows she covered had a higher quality of artwork.

Amanda closed her eyes. She so wanted the festival to be a success. Not so much for her, but for Connor and the entire community. Now with Desiree's harsh words out there for all to see, she worried about the fallout.

This was not the publicity she'd hoped for. But then she clung to a tiny hope. Maybe no one local would see it? Maybe it would get lost in the vast sea of social media posts? But even as the thought crossed her mind, she knew it was unlikely. In a close-knit community like Magnolia Key, news traveled quickly, and a review like this was bound to make waves.

She straightened in her chair and set her shoulders. She would not let one post on social media derail all the effort she and so many others had put into the festival. She clicked on another alert, her heart sinking when she discovered that a regional paper had shared Desiree's review on their social media account. That hadn't taken long…

A wave of guilt swept over her. As the organizer of the event, she couldn't help but feel responsible. She never should have contacted the art critic. If only she would have let it alone. But she'd been trying so hard to get more publicity for the festival.

Or had she been trying to get some acclaim for all she'd done? For her event-planning skills? The thought taunted her. Was she really that shallow? Had she gotten so used to the frequent accolades for her work that she craved to be noticed for all she'd done for Magnolia? The thought was sobering.

How had she let this happen? How had she let some snobby, big-city critic come and pan the art show? Amanda knew art and firmly believed there was unbelievable talent in the pieces selected for the show. She'd firmly believed that others would see the beauty and value in the work as she did.

So why had Desiree, with her haughty, big-city attitude, been so critical?

Her mind raced with thoughts of damage control. The last thing she wanted was for one critic's words to overshadow the hard work and dedication the artists had put into their work.

But most of all, she worried about Connor. The idea of him stumbling upon Desiree's post made her stomach churn. But Connor wasn't really a social media type guy. There was a good chance he would remain blissfully unaware of Desiree's harsh words.

She could only hope that this post would

fade away as most posts on social media do. And she fervently hoped that Connor never got wind of it.

Connor made his way to the hardware store in town, determined to find some oil to silence the incessant squeaking of the door to his cottage. The sound had been grating on his nerves, and despite his certainty that he had some oil somewhere, it had mysteriously vanished. But he wanted it fixed before Brooklyn showed up with her high energy and her tendency to dart in and out of the cottage.

As he entered the store, he nodded to the store owner—Jake, wasn't it? Then he surprised himself by speaking aloud. "Afternoon, Jake."

Jake's eyebrows lifted, clearly taken aback. "Ah… hi, Connor."

He couldn't fault Jake for his surprise. He rarely actually spoke to people when he shopped. He was more of a nodder.

Connor found the oil and went back up front, holding up the oil can. "Squeaky door."

"Yep, that happens. The salty air seems a bit rough on the hinges." Jake rang him out, then paused, holding the can mid-air. "Um… sorry about that review of the art show. I think it was pretty harsh. Sounds like it was written by someone who doesn't know what they're talking about. I was over at city hall and peeked in where Amanda was storing the artwork. Some pretty impressive pieces in there."

Connor had no idea what Jake was talking about. What review? And how was there a review when the show hadn't even happened yet? He'd thought the show was so small and local that it would fly under the radar of any art critics.

"Anyway, it was just that regional paper. Don't let it get to you." Jake handed him the oil.

All he did was nod as he turned and walked out of the store. He headed home, plopped down in front of his computer, and did a quick search on the Heritage Festival. Didn't take him long to find the post. He slowly read through it, his anger growing at each word. Not only had his work been panned, but all the other artwork had too. The review of his work had just been the harshest.

Then he noticed the name of the poster. Desiree Knight. He clenched his jaw. Looked like he was never going to get that woman out of his life. This was her revenge for what he did. Or more precisely, what he didn't do. He didn't do what she demanded of him. And then he'd left New York and Desiree and that whole life behind him.

But he was certain of one thing. He wasn't going to show his art at the festival's art show. Not if Amanda was going behind his back to bring in critics. He didn't need that. It had taken him long enough to get back to woodworking after what happened the last time. He didn't need Desiree's words playing over and over in his mind. And he certainly wouldn't trust his artwork to someone who never even told him that she was bringing in art critics. He thought this was a simple, local art show. That locals would see his work. He even thought it might lead to him placing some artwork in a local shop. That he was finally ready for that. But... not now. Not ever.

He pushed back from the table, the chair legs scraping on the floor. He strode over and opened the door—that still squeaked, but didn't annoy him half as much as he was annoyed with Amanda right now. No, past annoyed. He was furious with her.

He crossed the distance between their

cottages and rapped on her door. She opened it, looking surprised. She glanced at her watch. "You're early for dinner."

"How could you go behind my back like that?" He threw the words out at her, his hands balled into fists with his fingers digging into his palms.

She glanced at him warily. "What did I do?"

But he swore he saw a flicker in her eyes. She knew what she did.

"You had an art critic come and critique the art being displayed at the festival." He shook his head incredulously. "And you let her see it when it was crammed in that back room in city hall? What were you thinking? That was certainly not showing the art in its best light."

"Connor, I—"

He waved his hand. "Don't want to hear it. I never agreed to that. You said a small, local showing celebrating the island's heritage. Not that you were bringing in people to judge the work. And look what she said about the other work too. That most of it was unremarkable. Which is very wrong. There's some good, strong artistic talent there."

"I know. There is—"

He cut her off again. "Anyway, I'm pulling

out. There's no way I'm displaying my art at the show. I'm done. Finished. I'll go get my art piece and that's that."

"Connor, wait. Listen to me."

"There's nothing you can say. I trusted you with my art. You knew I hadn't shown anything in a very long time. And now this. I don't need the critique of my work. And I don't need to be around someone I can't trust to go behind my back—without saying a word to me—and arrange for this art critic to come."

"I'm sorry... You don't understand." Her eyes pleaded with him, and he ignored it.

"You're right. I don't understand. I don't understand how you could do this. You never said a word about it. Didn't talk to me about bringing in an art critic. And I had to find out about the review from someone else." He glared at her, his anger overwhelming him. "It's over, Amanda. All of it."

He swiveled around and crossed the distance in long, measured strides. Putting the art show behind him. Putting Amanda behind him. He'd been right to choose a reclusive life... because look what happened when he decided to trust people again.

~

Amanda slowly closed the door and wandered over to the table, sinking into a chair. Her gaze drifted across the carefully set table, all waiting for the intimate dinner she had planned. The dinner she would now eat alone. A hollow feeling settled in her chest. Not that she was hungry. She'd lost her appetite.

Connor's eyes had flashed with a scorching anger, turning an icy, inky blue. She hadn't in a million years thought a critic would pan his work. It was exquisite. So beautiful. It was like each piece held the soul of what he carved. The lines, the wood, the smooth, silky finish. Each piece was a masterpiece. She firmly believed that.

But... Desiree sure hadn't. Her review was brutal. But that couldn't have been the first non-glowing review Connor had ever gotten, could it? Don't all artists find people who don't click with their work and don't appreciate it?

But she did feel terrible. She'd felt certain Connor would ease his way back into showing his work and that he might be happy to see it reviewed. That the festival might be just his first step.

But now? After Desiree's remarks?

And had she done this for Connor? Or for herself? That idea still mocked her. Had she been wanting some accolades for herself too?

What if he gave up carving again? Could she have actually made that happen? Ruined his career by her eagerness to get his art out there again? She'd honestly wanted to show his art to the world, but she realized now that wasn't what Connor wanted. It was what she wanted *for* Connor. And it hadn't been her choice to make.

She let out a long sigh. And who knew which artists might pull their work out, just like Connor? She'd made a mess of things.

CHAPTER 22

Amanda went to Coastal Coffee early the next morning, seeking Beverly's guidance. Or a shoulder to cry on. Or something. She just couldn't stay in that cottage any longer, looking out the window, hoping to catch a glimpse of Connor.

As she slid into a chair, the familiar scents and sounds of the cafe did little to soothe her. While she waited for Beverly to finish up with a nearby table, she traced the grain on the worn wooden table. Beverly came over and handed her a mug of steaming coffee. "Here, this will help."

"How did you know I need help?"

"Your face looks like you lost your best friend."

Amanda's fingers instinctively curled around the warm mug. Beverly had no idea how close she was to the truth.

"I... I did something and Connor got really angry and pulled out of the art show." She couldn't hide the slight tremor in her voice. "And I'm afraid more people are going to pull out."

"You mean because of that online review?"

She looked up, surprised. "You heard about it too?"

"I reckon about everyone in town has heard about it. And you're right. They are mad."

"I knew it." She sighed with a weary resignation. "I've ruined everything. I've failed the town." And failed Connor...

"No, you haven't. Look at all you've done. We're going to have a bigger and better festival than we've had in years."

"They're all going to be so mad when they read the review."

Beverly shook her head slowly. "They aren't mad at you. They're mad at that Desiree woman. The consensus is that she's some snobby city woman who doesn't really know anything about handcrafted artwork."

"Really?" She looked up hopefully. "They aren't mad at me?"

"No one I've talked to is."

"Well, Connor sure is. He's mad I contacted an art critic to review the work. And furious that I gave a preview instead of waiting until it all could be set up at the pavilion to show all the work in its best light. He's right about that. I shouldn't have let her see the pieces in that cramped room."

"Ah, well. Lesson learned. And maybe Connor will come around."

"I doubt it. He was so angry. Enraged, boiling, seething. Oh, and livid." She smiled wryly. "Okay, I've run out of words to describe how furious he was. But he made it crystal clear he was done. With the art show, the festival… and with me."

"Oh, hon. I'm so sorry. Men can be so stubborn sometimes."

"I shouldn't have called the critic. I knew he was tentative about showing his art. And maybe… maybe I just did it so people would congratulate me on putting together such a great art show. I wanted to prove to everyone here on the island that I knew what I was doing. Only… obviously, I don't."

"You're too hard on yourself. Most people appreciate all you've done." Beverly's eyes filled with warm assurance. "And the naysayers? Well, we're not going to let them rain on our parade, are we? The festival is going to be wonderful, you'll see. It will all come together just like you've envisioned."

"I sure hope so." She managed a faint smile.

"I've got to catch that table. I'll be back."

Beverly walked away and Amanda stared unseeingly into the depths of her untouched coffee as if it held all the answers. Well, one answer was already known. Connor was furious with her, and she'd ruined their budding relationship.

She only hoped he didn't stop carving because of the harsh criticism. Guilt hammered through her. How had she let this happen?

CHAPTER 23

On Thursday, Megan and Brooklyn arrived in a flurry of activity, their presence instantly filling Connor's cottage with laughter and commotion. Brooklyn's curls bounced as she twirled and danced around the room chanting, "We're going to the festival. Festival. Festival."

"Brooklyn, inside voice, please," Megan pleaded as she hauled a suitcase inside.

"Here, let me get that for you." Connor reached for the bag.

"Thanks. Got one more trip out to the car. I swear Brooklyn packed enough for a two-week stay." Megan shook her head.

"Can we stay for two weeks?" Brooklyn's eyes lit up.

"No," Megan and Connor said in unison.

Megan looked at him questioningly. "Everything okay?"

"Sure. It's great." He offered a tight-lipped smile but knew his tone sounded unconvincing.

"Brooklyn, take that little bag of yours back to your room and unpack, okay?" Megan motioned to the pink backpack adorned with flowers and a purple unicorn.

Brooklyn grabbed the bag, slipped it over her shoulder with a grunt of effort, and raced off down the hall. "The festival. The festival," she chanted as she disappeared.

"Okay, now talk to me. Something's wrong. I can tell by the look on your face."

"Everything is fine." He shifted his weight, avoiding her eyes.

"Liar." She set her lips in a firm line.

"What are we? Six?" He rolled his eyes at Megan, but he knew she wouldn't let it go.

"You might as well tell me because you know I'll get it out of you." She stood with her hands on her hips and a stubborn jut to her chin, daring him to try to dodge her questions.

Connor held up a hand in defeat. "Okay, okay. I'm just not thrilled with the idea of going to the festival. I'd rather stay home."

She narrowed her eyes. "Why? You don't even want to go see your work in the art show?"

"About that…"

"Connor, what did you do?" She pinned him with a glare.

"I pulled out of the art show."

"Why in the world would you do that?"

He clenched his jaw. "I had my reasons."

"Well, I'm not budging until you tell me," she demanded.

He let out a long, labored sigh. "Okay, so Amanda arranged for an art critic to come see the artwork. A preview. At that cramped room at city hall, for Pete's sake. Who does that? Anyway… the review came out, and it was… harsh. Not only of my work, but she insulted everyone's work."

"So you let one bad review make you pull out of the show?" Her voice was full of either frustration or reproach, but he wasn't sure which. Or maybe it was both.

He looked directly at his sister. "It was by… Desiree…"

Realization and knowing flickered in Megan's eyes. "For crying out loud. Can that woman just get out of your life?"

"Evidently, not."

"But why would you let anything she says make you change your mind about showing your work?" Megan pressed, her mouth set in a firm frown.

"Don't you see? She panned everyone's work to get back at me." He tried to patiently explain all this to Megan so she'd understand. Agree with him.

"So you pulled out... so she won." Megan shook her head. "She's still trying to control your life. And by pulling out of the show... you let her pull your strings. Again."

"It's not like that." He glared at his sister, his voice taking on a hard edge. "And I'm mad at Amanda for going behind my back and arranging for an art critic to come. She never said anything about this being more than a simple, local art show."

"I wasn't aware the event coordinator had to get the okay from you for every decision she makes about promoting the event." Megan rolled her eyes. "Did you at least explain to Amanda why you were so upset? Your history with Desiree?"

"Nope. There's no need to. Things are over between Amanda and me."

Megan plopped down into a chair. "You are

the most stubborn, pig-headed man I've ever met," she chided, but the words held no real bite. She sighed. "It's like you work at making your life harder."

"Gee, thanks for the support, sis." His voice dripped with sarcasm. Why couldn't Megan understand? Desiree represented the part of the art world he'd worked so hard to put far behind him.

"I'm sure she wouldn't have contacted Desiree if she'd known about what happened before."

"Look, it doesn't matter. I didn't want to be in the show, anyway. And whatever was happening between Amanda and me? Or what was starting? It had no future. She lives in New York. And I'm perfectly fine with my life here on Magnolia. Nothing would make me move back to New York."

Megan eyed him closely. "Nothing?"

"Nothing." He nodded his head roughly. "So I'll go to the festival because of Brooklyn. But we're not going to the art show."

"I really think you should talk to Amanda. Explain it to her." Megan pushed off the chair and walked over to him, jabbing her finger at his chest. "And I don't think you should have pulled out of the show."

"Megs. This is my decision." He said the words more sharply than he'd intended. "Please, drop it," he added more gently. She was just being a protective sister and wanted the best for him. He knew that. But her constant opinions and advice just opened old wounds he wasn't ready to face.

Connor sat at the table long after Megan took Brooklyn out for a walk on the beach with the hopes of burning off some of Brooklyn's energy after their long drive. Megan's words looped through his mind, an endless chorus he couldn't silence.

And as much as he wanted her to back off, to give him space to process his own feelings, he couldn't deny she was right about some things she'd said. And it did annoy him that he was still dancing to Desiree's tune, still letting her get under his skin and influence his decisions.

A sharp rap at his door brought Connor out of his thoughts. He got up from the table where he'd been shuffling papers, pretending to do paperwork. Why was Megan knocking? And why was she back so soon? She'd promised to take Brooklyn to the ice cream shop after their walk. He tugged the door open and his eyes widened in surprise at the unexpected visitor.

The woman people called Miss Eleanor stood on his front step, a determined expression on her face. Why *Miss Eleanor* and not *Mrs. Whatever-her-last-name-was* was beyond him.

"Mr. Dempsey. I'd like to speak with you." It was clear she wasn't asking his permission.

"Yes, ma'am." He nodded, his manners kicking in automatically. "Would you care to come in?"

"No, this is fine." She stood perfectly erect, a firm set to her shoulders. "We haven't even been formally introduced." She shoved her hand out. "Eleanor Griffin."

He shook her hand, then slipped his hand back into his pocket, unsure of what to expect from this impromptu visit.

"Now, what is this I hear about you pulling your artwork out of the show?"

"I… uh…" He stammered, taken aback by her directness. Why was it any of this woman's business? Was everyone going to be on his case about things that were his decisions to make?

She waved a hand. "I know you like your privacy. I get that," she continued, her voice softening slightly. "I admit I like mine too. But I saw that carving you did, and it was... exquisite. You're very talented, Mr. Dempsey. Your work has a unique quality that captures the essence of our small little town."

"Thank you." But it still was his decision to show his art or not. Even if everyone thought they had a say in it.

"That Desiree woman doesn't know what she's talking about," Miss Eleanor said, her tone sharp. "She obviously doesn't appreciate the real talent that went into all the work in the show. I don't think you should let one review cause you to withdraw from the show. Your art deserves to be seen and appreciated by the community."

"It's more complicated than that." He didn't feel like delving into the personal reasons behind his decisions, especially not with a near stranger.

"Is it?" She arched a brow, her expression skeptical. "You're a local artist. We need local artists to display their work at the festival. The festival is a celebration of the town. And our history. And what we've become now. Our local art is an important part of that. It showcases the talent and creativity that thrives here."

"But I—"

She waved her hand again. "You can make excuses if you want. But the town needs you. And you should want to show your work. It's lovely. I saw it once on display at a gallery in New York City when I was visiting there."

"You did?" The fact that she remembered seeing his work in the city years ago and remembered him caught him off guard.

"I did. You have a great talent, and it seems like a shame to hide it. It's beautiful and you should be very proud of your work. I want you to at least think about putting your work back in the show."

He nodded slowly, unable to resist the force of her impassioned words.

"And I know you've been dating Miss Kingston." The change in subject was so unexpected he could hardly register it before she continued. "It would be unfortunate to let this situation jeopardize your relationship. She's a remarkable woman, and she's done so much for this town. We should all be supportive." She gave him a meaningful glance.

"I… I'll give it some thought."

She turned to leave, paused, and then faced him once more. "And you'd be a fool to let one person's opinion change the course of your life."

With those parting words, she descended the stairs and marched off down the sidewalk.

Eleanor Griffin was a force to be reckoned with.

And was she right? Was Megan right? Had he made a big mistake? He scrubbed his hand over his face. Why had he let Desiree push his buttons? Let her get under his skin? Yet again.

He knew he was a better man than this. He was.

His heart sank as guilt washed over him. And look what he'd done to Amanda. Pulled out of the show when she was depending on him. Accused her of going behind his back when she had no idea of his history with Desiree.

Megan and Brooklyn approached, strolling up the sidewalk hand in hand. The remnant of Brooklyn's chocolate ice cream was smeared across the front of her shirt. "Uncle Connor. We had the bestest ice cream."

He chuckled. "I can see that."

Megan, however, looked at him closely. "You okay?"

"You're always asking me that."

"Because I'm always worried about you," she replied, her tone gentle but firm.

Brooklyn, oblivious to the undercurrent of tension, chimed in eagerly, "Guess what, Uncle Connor? We saw Miss Amanda, and she was working in the pavilion. She said she was getting stuff ready for tomorrow. The festival's tomorrow, you know. We're going, right? I can't wait."

"We're going, Princess." He turned to his sister. "Can I leave you two alone for a bit? I have somewhere I need to be."

A knowing grin spread across Megan's face. "I hope it involves going to the pavilion."

He grinned back at her. "It just might. And you won't hear me say this again, but you were right. I have been a fool."

"Told you so." Megan laughed and gave him a nudge. "Go fix your mess. We'll be here when you get back."

CHAPTER 24

Amanda struggled with the heavy wooden backdrop, trying to maneuver it into position. Her arms ached from the effort, and she wished she had asked for help. As she pushed and pulled, she suddenly felt the weight of the backdrop ease. Looking up, she saw Connor holding the other end, his strong hands gripping the wood firmly.

"Need a hand?" he asked, his blue eyes meeting hers.

She nodded, surprised to see him. They worked together silently, moving the backdrop into place. Once it was settled, Amanda stepped back, brushing a strand of hair from her face with the back of her hand.

"Thanks," she said, uncertain of why he was

here. He'd made it clear he wanted nothing to do with the festival… or with her.

"Can we talk?" He shifted uneasily on his feet.

"I thought you'd pretty much said everything there was to say." She crossed her arms, unconsciously adopting a defensive posture as conflicting emotions swirled within her. Part of her still stung from his abrupt rejection.

"Look, I…" He took a step toward her. "I… I want to apologize for how I reacted. For the things I said to you. I shouldn't have gotten so angry."

Surprise swept through her at his words, but she remained silent, letting him continue.

He took another step closer. "Let me explain. Please. It's not just about the harsh review. It's about my past, and the reasons I left New York in the first place."

She nodded, sensing that Connor needed to tell his story in his own time.

"When I was younger and living in New York, my art caught the eye of a prominent gallery owner. I started to make a name for myself. But… I trusted the wrong people. Desiree was one of them."

Her eyes widened. "You know Desiree?"

"I do. She was involved in the art world back then, not as a critic, but as a buyer. She knew everyone who was anyone. And I thought she was my friend. She gave me advice, and I listened to her. I was young and foolish."

"What happened?" she asked softly, drawn into his tale by the raw emotion breaking through in his voice.

"She encouraged me to sell a handful of my pieces to a company. I didn't have a lawyer look over the contract and Desiree assured me everything was fine. But then, as I got more well-known, the company took my art and mass-produced it. Like the kind of cheap wood knickknack you'd see in a tourist trap."

"I'm so sorry." Amanda could see the pain in his eyes, knowing full well the importance he placed on the authenticity of his craft. Her heart ached for him.

"I was consumed by anger, but found out that I'd unwittingly signed my rights away to those pieces and any replica of them. Desiree thought it was no big deal. She even thought I should sell them more pieces. But that's... that's not what my art is."

"Of course not."

"Then a smaller gallery showed some of those mass-produced pieces, trying to cash in on my name. As those pieces began to flood the market, the value of my real artwork dropped significantly." His eyes glinted with anger and frustration. "I got fewer requests for gallery showings. Disillusioned with the whole art scene in New York, I finally decided to leave. Desiree ridiculed me for leaving and not giving over more of my work. She called it easy money."

"Desiree was wrong. Your artwork is one of a kind." She took a step toward him and took his hands in hers. "I wish I had known all this."

"That's what Megan said. That none of this is your fault. And that I should explain why I was so angry. It was just Desiree messing with my life again. And taking down the other people who were showing their art at the festival, victims of my past with Desiree. They didn't deserve that. She never even gave them a fair review."

"I'm glad Megan encouraged you to come talk to me. I understand so much better now."

"It wasn't just Megan," he smiled sheepishly. "Miss Eleanor came and talked to me too. She said I was a fool for letting one review sway my decision-making."

Amanda laughed. "Miss Eleanor is wise and opinionated. And she's never one to shy away from speaking her mind."

He looked straight into her eyes. "Will you forgive me for the way I acted?"

"I do forgive you now that I understand." The words came easily, and a surprising sense of relief washed over her.

"Do you think there's still room for my artwork in the show?"

"Of course there is."

"And what about us? Have I ruined everything? I don't blame you if you don't trust me anymore."

Did she trust him? She looked at him for a long moment. "I was hurt when you cut me off like that. I admit it." She swallowed hard, laying her heart on the line. "I thought we had... something... between us."

"We did. We do. If you'll give me another chance."

She reached up and touched his face, feeling the hint of whiskers beneath her fingertips as she traced his cheek. "I'd like nothing more than to start over with you. Try this again."

Connor broke into a wide grin and swept her off her feet, twirling her around in circles.

After he set her down, he pulled her into his arms, holding her tight. "Thank you for forgiving me. And for giving us another chance."

She leaned against him, drinking in his strength and his warmth. She tilted her head up to look at him, and he kissed her gently before stepping back. "Now, how about I help you get all this ready? And I'll be here first thing in the morning to set up the actual artwork."

CHAPTER 25

J ust like he said, Connor was there bright and early to help her set up the art show, greeting her with a wide smile and a quick kiss. He moved around the pavilion, adjusting the art with a keen eye. He stood back, tilting his head slightly as he eyed the display, making a few more tweaks until he was satisfied. She admired his attention to detail and dedication to making sure everything looked perfect.

Beverly showed up with Dale and Maxine, and they set up the display of historical items, asking Connor for his input to help arrange things. Amanda finally stood back and surveyed their work. "I think everything looks wonderful."

"You did such a good job with this," Beverly said as she came over and draped an arm around Amanda's waist and gave her a hug. "You should be proud of yourself."

"I just hope it all goes off without a hitch. At least the weather is cooperating." She looked up at the clear blue sky. "Couldn't ask for better weather."

"It wouldn't dare mess with our festival," Beverly said as more vendors began to arrive and set up along the boardwalk.

"I need to go check and see if anyone needs anything." She glanced over and grinned when she saw the funnel cake vendor setting up close by. She'd managed to snag a replacement funnel cake vendor with Beverly's help.

"I better run back to the cottage and get Megan and Brooklyn. I'll see you in a bit?" Connor squeezed her hand.

"Okay, see you soon." Her heart fluttered at the lingering glance he gave her before he turned and left.

Beverly turned to her and grinned. "Looks like you two worked things out."

Her cheeks warmed. "We did."

"Glad to see the man came to his senses."

Beverly nodded. "I better go. We're serving sandwiches at the cafe today. Expecting a brisk business. But I'll catch up with you tonight for the fireworks."

Amanda surveyed the bustling festival as she went to each vendor to make sure they were all set. People began to flood the area. Locals mingled with tourists. The ferry had set up extra trips back and forth for the day.

"Miss Kingston?" A man in a white suit stopped her and smiled. "We got our fourth singer. We're all set."

She smiled at him. "Oh, good. The festival wouldn't be the same without the barbershop quartet."

Amanda barely had time to enjoy the Heritage Festival as she ran around making sure everything was going smoothly. Connor, Megan, and Brooklyn finally caught up with her.

"You should take a break and enjoy yourself," Connor said. "After you put in all this work, you should at least get to experience it."

"I could be persuaded to indulge in some funnel cake." She laughed.

"Me too." Brooklyn jumped up and down. "Me too. Can I, Momma?"

"How about you split one with Uncle Connor?"

"I guess so." She scowled and turned to Connor. "You better not eat it all."

He ruffled her hair. "I won't, Princess, I promise."

Brooklyn took her uncle's hand and skipped by his side. She and Megan lagged behind them. "So, my brother finally told you what happened, huh?"

"He did. And I'm so sorry. I can see why he moved here and avoided the whole art scene."

"But his work should be seen. I hate that he hides it."

"Maybe showing it here at the show will make him more open to the idea."

"I certainly hope so."

Connor and Brooklyn returned with the funnel cakes and they took bites of them as they wandered along the weathered boardwalk. When they finished, Megan said, "Let's go see the art show now. I can't wait to see your work on display."

"Yes, Uncle Connor is famous now." Brooklyn bobbed her head.

"Not quite, Princess."

They walked over to the pavilion, and Miss

Eleanor stopped them. "Amanda, you've done a fine job with the festival." She looked at Connor, then Amanda, and a small smile crept across her lips. "Just wanted to let you know." She turned to leave, but not before nodding at Connor approvingly.

"I think she's pleased you listened to her," Amanda whispered.

"I'm pretty sure everyone in town does what Miss Eleanor asks." He grinned back at her.

They climbed the stairs to the pavilion and browsed through the artwork and historical items. When they got in front of Connor's carvings, a man standing looking at the carvings turned around. "These are original Connor Dempsey carvings."

"They are." Amanda nodded.

"You can tell because he signs his work with these carved symbols on the bottom. Do you know where I can contact him? I'd like to see some of his newer work."

Connor's eyes narrowed. "Why?"

"My wife is a collector of his work. I'd love to surprise her with a new piece for our fiftieth wedding anniversary. I bought one of his carvings earlier at a small cafe in town. But I was so eager to show her that I already gave it to her. Now I find myself without a fiftieth wedding anniversary present."

Amanda turned to Connor, not giving him away. Megan nudged him with a gentle bump.

Connor held out his hand. "I'm Connor Dempsey. Pleased to meet you."

"You are? Wonderful." The man pumped Connor's hand. "This is great."

"Maybe you could come by my workshop and see some of my new work. We'll see if we can find something your wife might like."

"That's great. I'll be back in town next week. Will that work?"

"It will."

"Perfect." The man smiled and walked away.

"See, told you people want your art," Megan said pointedly.

"And you're always right, aren't you, Megs?"

"Pretty much." Megan took Brooklyn's hand. "How about we go see what kind of sandwiches Miss Beverly has? We'll meet you two back here in a bit." They took off with Brooklyn taking a skip and a hop for each of Megan's steps. It was just a simple moment, but it warmed Amanda's heart. It was moments like these that made Magnolia Key feel like home, a place where dreams could blossom and hope take flight.

She pulled her gaze from Megan and Brooklyn and turned to Connor. "Are you... happy? Are you ready to sell your art again?"

"I'm not sure how I feel. Been a long time since I sold a piece."

"Maybe it's time to get back in the art world." She squeezed his hand. "If you think you're ready. If it's something you want."

"Maybe it is."

Beverly came by later, all smiles. "Biggest turnout we've ever had for the festival. Everyone is so pleased. You did a wonderful job."

"Thank you. I was glad I was here to help."

"Is it just like the one you went to when you were a girl?"

She looked up at Connor, then back to Beverly. "Pretty much." She grinned. "But a few changes."

Connor grinned, and Beverly laughed. "Nothing wrong with a few changes. Good changes." Beverly shook her head. "Things have a way of working out here on Magnolia. Anyway, I better run. Meeting up with Maxine and Dale. Oh, and I'll take down all the history items after the fireworks, don't worry about those. I've wrangled some volunteers to take the art back to city hall, too. The artists can pick up their work there. Oh, and so far, the auction has brought in more than ever. The funding for next year's festival is secure."

"Oh, I'm so glad." A pang of melancholy struck her. Not that she'd be there, but at least whoever took over next year wouldn't have to worry about funds.

They met up later with Megan and Brooklyn and sat on the wall near the boardwalk and watched the fireworks. The crowd oohed and aahed as the display lit up the sky. Each shower of glittering embers reminded her of the magic this island had brought to her life. The grand finale was a masterpiece of colors and booms and sparkles. She snuck a look at Connor, the lights reflecting in his eyes. He turned and smiled at her before looking up at the display again. Joy rose in her, filling her with a sense of contentment. What had begun as a simple respite from the hustle of her city life had become so much more.

After the show, they all headed back to the cottages. Brooklyn yawned, no longer her energetic, skipping self. Connor scooped her up in his arms and carried her the rest of the way.

When they got to his cottage, Megan took Brooklyn. "I better get her to bed. Good night, Amanda. It was a wonderful festival."

"Thank you."

Megan and Brooklyn slipped into Connor's cottage, and he took Amanda's hand, leading her over to hers. They climbed her deck slowly.

"I've been wanting to kiss you all day." His eyes twinkled like the fireworks.

"What a coincidence. I've been wanting to be kissed all day."

He took her into his arms, kissing her gently. She sighed, feeling like she was right where she belonged.

Beverly and Maxine worked at the pavilion after the fireworks, packing up items. She turned when she felt someone watching her. "Cliff, what are you doing here?"

"I wanted to talk to you. I came earlier and looked at the items you have here in the historical display."

Maxine came to stand beside her. "Cliff, we're kind of busy now."

He nodded over to where the purse and the

letter still rested on the table with the painting she'd found in her office propped up behind it. She'd placed a sign near them asking anyone who knew anything about the items to contact her. "You know how you were hoping someone had some idea to help you with unraveling some of the mystery from the items you found? I can't really help with the painting, but I can with the letter."

Beverly eyed him suspiciously, doubting she should trust him, but curious anyway. "You can?"

"It's in code."

Maxine snapped her fingers. "That's what we thought."

"We already figured that, Cliff."

"I know the code," he said simply.

"How?" She frowned.

"My grandmother taught it to me. Kind of a family secret, I guess."

"And your mother knows it?"

"I'm sure she does."

"That's why Miss Eleanor was so cryptic when she saw the letter," Maxine said. "So what does it say?"

"It says meet me at the landing at seven Friday night."

"It does?" Beverly walked over and picked up the letter, looking at the random words on the page.

"It does. Don't know who wrote it. But that's what it says."

She looked at Cliff for a moment. "Well… thank you. At least that's something to go on."

"Can I help you take all this down?"

She stared at him for a long moment. "No, I don't think so. I don't need your help." Not with packing up the art and the historical items, not with anything.

Cliff let out a sigh. "Okay, but someday you're going to have to talk to me. We should sort things out."

"There is nothing to sort out, Cliff. Nothing."

He nodded once, then turned and walked away. Maxine wrapped her arm around her waist. "You okay?"

"I am. He just… gets under my skin, and I shouldn't let him."

"I guess the festival brought him back to town." Maxine looked over to where Cliff was heading down the boardwalk.

"I guess. Or trying to get more people on his

side about his ridiculous high-rise at the end of the boardwalk." Beverly scowled.

"We won't let that happen. Miss Eleanor won't let it happen. Maybe she can talk some sense into her son."

"I'm not sure that Cliff ever listens to anyone."

CHAPTER 26

T he next day, Megan and Brooklyn packed up to head home. Amanda went over to say goodbye to them.

"Miss Amanda, the festival was fun, wasn't it? I can't wait for next year. Do I really have to wait that long? I hope I don't have to wait that long to see fireworks again. Weren't they the bestest?"

"The festival was fun. I'm glad you had such a good time." It reminded her of how excited she'd been to go to the festival when she was a young girl. Asking her father to bring her back the next year. And her dad had promised her he would. But that never happened.

But yesterday, she'd felt his presence strongly

as she walked around the festival as if he was there and watching her enjoy it again.

"Brooklyn, grab your backpack." Megan's voice broke through her nostalgic memories. "We need to run. I want to catch the next ferry."

"I want to stay here with Uncle Connor. I want to live on Magnolia Island forever."

"That would be nice, Princess, but your mom has a job and a life back on the mainland."

"She should find one here, like you did."

"It's pretty hard to find a job in a small town."

Brooklyn kicked at the sand in the driveway. "It would be more funner to live here with you. We could see you all the time."

Megan laughed. "Your uncle would never get any work done if you were here, Brookie."

"I still think it's a good idea." Brooklyn scowled as she climbed into the car. "Bye, Uncle Connor. Bye, Miss Amanda."

Megan hugged her. "We did have a fabulous time. Thank you for making that possible." Then she leaned in closer and whispered, "Good luck with my brother. You'll need to be patient with him. But he's a really great guy."

"He is and I will." She hugged Megan back.

Megan and Brooklyn drove off, and Connor turned to her, taking in a deep breath. "I do love that little girl, but she sure has boundless energy."

"She does. Any bets on whether she talks Megan into moving here?"

"Doubt she'd win that one. Megs loves her job. And they're close enough to visit often. It'll be easier when the bridge is finished."

"When is it supposed to be finished?"

"Next year sometime? I think." He took her hand. "How about a play date today with your favorite neighbor? Picnic on the beach? Some swimming?"

"A play date sounds wonderful. I need some time to decompress. Let me go slip on my suit and I'll make up some sandwiches or something."

"A step ahead of you. I've already got the picnic made." He grinned. "Okay, Megan helped me."

She was back outside in ten minutes, sunscreen carefully applied and a bright teal coverup over her swimsuit. Connor set up a cozy oasis beneath a pop-up canopy, with a large bright blanket, a stack of towels, a cooler with soda, and a picnic basket open with a peek of the goodies inside.

"Look at you all prepared." She sank down beside him.

"I'm trying to impress my neighbor." He winked at her.

"She's dutifully impressed."

He jumped up. "How about a swim before we eat?" He reached down a hand and pulled her effortlessly to her feet.

She stood beside him on the sand, grinned, and then pushed him backward as he stumbled slightly. "Last one to the water loses." She raced across the sand and laughed when she felt him scoop her up in his arms as he plunged into the water.

"Put me down." She laughed.

"You don't play fair. So now you go swimming." He kept walking deeper, then tossed her into the water. She came up sputtering and laughing, the warm water caressing her skin.

"Hey." She swung her arm in a circle, throwing an arc of water at him.

Soon they were embroiled in a water fight like two kids Brooklyn's age. She dunked him. He tossed her. They splashed. The cares that so often had weighed her down dissipated with the rolling waves and warm sunshine. Soon, exhausted, they headed up to the pop-up, grabbed towels, and dropped down on the beach blanket.

She couldn't remember having this much fun in a long time. Just easy-going laughter, teasing, and… just plain fun.

He pulled a plate of tiny triangle sandwiches out of the basket. Connor said Brooklyn helped make them, which explained how some of them were squished. They also had fruit, cheese, and crackers, and finished off with pieces of a pecan pie Megan had made, its buttery, nutty flavor the perfect end to the picnic.

They packed up their things, and Connor turned to her. "Want to come over and watch the sunset?"

"That sounds nice. Let me grab a quick shower to rinse off the sand and saltwater. I'll be over soon."

She hurried to her cottage and showered, then slipped on a pair of capris and a pink knit shirt. Her attire here on the island had slowly evolved into brighter, more casual clothes with the help of numerous shopping trips to the local stores. She decided to let her hair dry naturally —something she never would have done in New

York where she used her expensive, fancy hair dryer and curling iron daily. But this slower, more relaxed lifestyle was growing on her.

She headed back to Connor's, and he was waiting for her on his deck with a chilled bottle of wine and the lanterns lit with flickering candles. "Connor, you really can drink beer, you know."

"I know. But I've become accustomed to sharing a bottle of wine with you."

They watched the sky come alive with colors as if it was competing with last night's fireworks, brilliant in its own way. The stars began to blink into existence. Beside her on the glider, Connor's solid presence warmed her, and she instinctively leaned against him, their fingers intertwining. Even though they didn't say much, she could feel the connection with him. A deep connection that felt so right. Yet the looming reality of her life back in the city threatened to shatter the magic.

"Connor—"

"Amanda—"

They both laughed. "You first," he said.

"I was just going to say that… you've made my time in Magnolia so special. I love spending time with you."

His fingers traced the curve of her cheek, his touch gentle yet charged with an undeniable electricity. "And my time with you has been special too." His gaze held hers with an intensity that made her heart skip. He wrapped his arm around her shoulder and she snuggled against him, wanting to freeze the moment.

"I feel like Brooklyn wishing I could stay here forever."

"I wish you could too," he said softly, his voice laced with longing.

Later when he walked her back to her cottage, he gave her a lingering kiss filled with a bittersweet promise. Back inside her cozy cottage, her mind whirled with possibilities. An idea began to form. More of a wish, really. A fleeting, tantalizing dream.

What if she did stay longer here in Magnolia?

But what about her company, her business? She really couldn't stay away from New York much longer and expect to have a business to go back to.

CHAPTER 27

The next morning, Amanda woke up with a smile on her face, remembering the last few days. The success of the festival. Brooklyn's enthusiasm for life. And Connor, of course. He was never far from her thoughts.

She brewed a pot of coffee and took a steaming mug over to the table. Opening her laptop, she still wondered if she could delay her return to New York. She wasn't ready for this magical time to end.

She was greeted with the familiar, unending stream of messages. Although she had to admit there were fewer coming in as the weeks went by. She opened one and read it, sensing the urgency and pleading in the woman's words. It was an offer—more like a heartfelt plea—to run a big fundraiser for Alzheimer's research. Her heart leaped with the opportunity to do something for the cause. If only more research had been done before Nana had succumbed to the disease. And she didn't wish for anyone to have to go through what Nana did.

How could she turn this down? A cause that was near and dear to her heart. A chance to make a difference. But was she ready to return to the city? She'd need to soon to get started on it.

She closed her laptop, unable or unwilling to make a decision. All she could think of were Brooklyn's words. "I want to stay here on Magnolia forever."

And she agreed with the girl's sentiment. But she had real life to get back to. Her thoughts warred with each other. Her desire to stay here and her need to get back to New York.

With a sigh, she hurried to get dressed, her mind swirling with conflicted thoughts. She headed to Coastal Coffee in need of a talk with Beverly. Somehow, talking with Beverly always helped bring her clarity.

And who are you going to talk to in New York? Her thoughts taunted her, reminding her of the loneliness awaiting her back in the city. She shoved them aside and walked over to the cafe, slipping inside, embracing the familiarity of it. The aroma, the sounds, the sights.

"Amanda, over here." Beverly waved her over to where she was talking to Miss Eleanor. "So, have you recovered from everything? Such a lot of work you've put in. I bet it's nice to have that behind you."

"And you did a good job. You're so organized. I bet you can do anything you put your mind to," Miss Eleanor said as she poured a generous amount of cream into her coffee.

"I—it was a lot. And I'm glad it all worked out."

Beverly frowned. "Then why don't you look pleased?"

Miss Eleanor double-tapped the table. "Sit down. Talk."

Amanda did as Miss Eleanor commanded. "It's just... I've loved my time here on the island. Loved working on the festival and getting to know so many people."

"Like Connor," Miss Eleanor said pointedly.

"Yes, Connor. And Beverly. And Tori and... well, everyone."

"So, what's the problem?" Beverly asked.

"I got asked to run a big gala in New York.

A fundraiser for Alzheimer's. It's a cause I really believe in." She could hear the excitement and hesitation in her own voice.

"But you're not ready to leave?" Miss Eleanor pinned her with a hard look.

Her shoulders sagged. "I had just been thinking about extending my stay. I'm not sure I'm ready to face all the chaos that's city life. But this event could really use my help." She shrugged. "I have no idea what to do. I know I eventually need to return to New York or I won't have a career anymore."

Miss Eleanor reached over, her weathered hand enveloping Amanda's. "You need to do what your heart tells you to do. Listen to it. Because if you don't, you'll regret it your whole life. I know this. And it's a hard life lesson to learn." A hint of distant regret flickered across the woman's eyes.

"Listen to Miss Eleanor. She's a wise woman who's seen more than her fair share of life's twists and turns." Beverly nodded. "You'll have to figure out what you truly want and have the courage to follow that path."

Amanda headed back to her cottage, slowly winding her way along the now familiar streets. She walked in and out of the sunshine, feeling it wash over her. The gentle breeze blew her hair around her shoulders as the salt air caressed her skin. None of that was making it easier to decide.

She got to her cozy cottage, passing through the living area and out to the deck. She took in the vast expanse stretched out before her. The waves rolling to shore. The bird flying overhead. The sun sparkling like diamonds on the water. So in contrast to the view of towering buildings and bustling streets out her apartment window.

"Hey, you." The familiar voice broke through her thoughts as Connor jogged up to her porch and climbed the stairs. "Came looking for you earlier, but you weren't here."

"I went to see Beverly."

He studied her intently. "Is something wrong?"

"No." She frowned. "Yes."

He took her hand in his strong, calloused one. "Talk to me."

She drew in a deep breath. "I… I got a job offer. One I'd really like to take. It's for a fundraising gala for Alzheimer's research."

A crestfallen look crossed his features, but he quickly recovered, offering her a reassuring squeeze of his hand. "But that's good, right? You'd be helping out with a cause I know you believe in."

"But... I'd have to leave Magnolia. I'd have to leave soon." She reached up and touched his face. A face that had become so comfortingly familiar to her over the last months. "I'm... I'm not sure I'm ready to leave. To give up my life here on the island."

"Selfishly, I'd love for you to stay." His blue eyes filled with tenderness and longing. "But I know your career is in New York. I understand. And I know this cause is important to you."

She felt a pang in her chest as she looked out over the rolling waves gently lapping the shoreline. "It is. I'd love to help them. See if they can bring in substantial funding for the much-needed research."

He pushed a lock of hair away from her face. "It kind of sounds like you've made your decision."

"Maybe I have." She sighed, her heart breaking. "But I feel like it's a no-win decision. If I stay here longer, I have to give up planning the fundraiser. If I do the fundraiser, I have to leave Magnolia."

Connor held her close, his hand lightly tracing soothing circles on her back. "Sometimes life causes us to make hard decisions. Where we have to choose between two things and neither one is the perfect option."

Her heart swelled with a bittersweet ache as she contemplated the decision before her. Memories of her beloved Nana's warm, loving spirit and staunch devotion flooded her mind, quickly followed by the cruel reality of Alzheimer's that had slowly stolen her away. In those final years, she'd witnessed firsthand the devastating toll the disease took, ravaging both mind and body until her cherished Nana was but a shell of her former self.

She knew in her heart that she couldn't pass up the chance to work on the Alzheimer's event. Not after everything Nana had done for her. If raising funds for research made it that much closer until a cure was found, that was what she needed to do.

"You're going, aren't you?" he asked, gently.

"I think I have to."

"I know," he said softly as he wrapped his arms around her and held her close.

CHAPTER 28

B ack in New York, Amanda struggled to slip back into the familiar rhythm of her former routine. She yearned for her life on Magnolia Key. She missed her life there. Missed the warmth of Beverly's easy smile, Tori's enthusiasm about her theater, and even missed Miss Eleanor telling her what to do.

And, of course, she missed Connor. He called her often, but their conversations became more and more strained as distance and time stretched between them.

She threw herself into her work. Answering constant text messages and emails. Arranging flowers with painstaking precision and menu choices with utmost care. She checked regularly with the venue to ensure it could accommodate their ever-growing list of gala attendees. People were paying handsomely for a coveted seat at one of the tables, and the highly anticipated auction promised to be a lucrative affair. She worked tirelessly on getting more donations for the auction, determined to make sure they raised as much as possible. Giving hope to families who struggled with a loved one with Alzheimer's.

Miss Eleanor's words rang through her mind. Follow her heart. And she thought she had. But as loneliness engulfed her and the hectic life in the city swallowed her whole again, she wasn't certain.

She looked at her watch, seeing that once again she'd worked through dinner without taking a break. She should really wrap things up and head home for the evening. She cleared up her desk—but not without stuffing a handful of work into her bag along with her heavy leather binder. She flicked off the light and left her office. An office that had a desk that cost way too much, and rich leather chairs for people to sit in. There was also a conference room precisely decorated by a well-known designer where she could meet with clients. All this that used to please her didn't anymore.

She left her office and took the elevator down to the lobby. The ever-present attendant at the reception desk greeted her. "Miss Kingston, there's a gentleman waiting to see you. I told him you hadn't left yet, but he didn't want to disturb your work." The attendant gestured across the expansive lobby.

She turned, and her breath caught in her throat. "Connor." She flew across the distance and flung herself into his arms, not caring if anyone was watching, just wanting to feel his arms around her.

He held her close, his chin resting on her head, then leaned down to capture her lips in a tender kiss. "I've missed you," he murmured.

"Oh, I've missed you." She stood on tiptoes and kissed him again. "What are you doing here?"

"I have a meeting here in the city at… an art gallery. They want to showcase my work at an upcoming exhibition." There was pride in his voice but also a bit of hesitancy.

"Connor, that's wonderful news." She hugged him.

Then his face turned somber. "And I came to see you. We need to talk." The look on his face worried her.

"Okay, but not here. Come back to my apartment. It's not far."

They stepped out onto the bustling sidewalk, blending in with the sea of anonymous people passing by. Nothing like back in Magnolia, where people would call out cheery hellos as they passed.

She let him into her apartment, and he looked around the space. "Not what I expected," he admitted, his gaze taking in her sleek, modern furnishing.

She sighed and kicked off her shoes. "I know. It's not me, is it?"

"I'm not sure. I don't really know the New York version of you."

"I'm still just me." But was she? Here in the city where she rushed around, ignored people in the street, and never took a moment to look up. She frowned as she crossed over to the floor-to-ceiling windows and peered out, trying to get a glimpse of the night sky between the buildings.

She turned back to Connor, who stood awkwardly in her sterile apartment. "Come here, sit down." She crossed over to the couch and tucked her legs under her. He came over and sat at the end of the couch, looking uncomfortable and out of place. But then, the couch was uncomfortable, wasn't it? It looked stylish, but who in their right mind picked style over comfort?

She had, she thought ruefully.

"So you wanted to talk?" She looked at him sitting straight and rigid on the couch, dreading what was coming.

"This isn't working for me." He met her gaze steadily.

Her heart sank. She knew it. But how could she blame him when they lived twelve hundred miles apart?

"There was something between us, right? You felt it?" he asked, watching her closely.

"Yes, there was…. There still is." She paused. "At least for me."

"Good." He bobbed his head, the corners of his mouth lifting into a tentative smile. "Then we'll need to solve this distance thing, won't we?"

She frowned again, not sure how you could move Florida closer to New York.

"I was thinking." He leaned forward. "I could… move back to New York."

Her eyes widened, his suggestion catching her off guard. "You'd be willing to move back here?"

He scooted across the couch, right next to her, close enough that she could feel his warmth. "I'd do about anything to be back with you again. Where I see you every day. Where I can kiss you when I want." He kissed her just to prove his point.

She melted into the kiss, savoring his touch, before reluctantly pulling back. "But you said you'd never move back to the city. You love your life on Magnolia."

"I do. But if it means we can't be together… well then, living there doesn't work for me."

"You'd give up all that for me?"

"Don't you realize by now?" He reached out, his calloused fingertips grazing her cheek. "I love you, Amanda Kingston. I'm hopelessly in love with you. I don't want to spend another minute apart from you."

She sat there stunned, his words rendering her momentarily speechless. "You… love me?"

"Very much."

"I love you too." The words spilled out as she threw her arms around him and buried her face in his neck, her tears falling on his skin.

He reached down and wiped her tears away. "So… you're all in on this?"

"I'm all in. I've never been more all in on

anything in my life." She sat back. "Only we have a problem."

"What's that?" He narrowed his eyes warily.

"I don't want to live in New York. Not anymore." The realization had been brewing within her for weeks now.

"You don't?" His eyes widened. "But I thought—"

She shook her head, cutting him off gently. "Yeah, I thought so too. But I don't want to live here anymore. I do have to finish up my work on the gala. I've already committed to that. But there is too much noise and commotion and constant demands here. Once I saw how life could be on Magnolia Key, I wanted that for me. I crave it."

"You do? But your business?"

"There are events everywhere, not just in New York. And I've actually had a competitor reach out to me, wanting to buy into my business. It would be a good way to transition out of it. I'd have to make some trips back here to New York, but I'd mostly work remotely."

"I could come with you and check on my work in the galleries here." A wide smile spread across his face. "I think we could make this work."

"And there are other ways I can use my skills to help raise funds for research for Alzheimer's."

"You'd really be happy living in Magnolia?"

"I would. I know I would." She'd never been more certain of anything in her life.

"I have to admit, I'm kind of glad I don't have to move back here to this concrete jungle." He chuckled, his eyes twinkling.

"And I'm kind of glad I don't have to stay here anymore."

"Come home as soon as you can, will you?"

"I will. I promise." She curled up in his arms, right where she belonged.

CHAPTER 29

Connor made frequent trips to New York to visit Amanda, and then she moved back to Magnolia as soon as the gala finished. Brooklyn and Megan were at his cottage when she arrived, and Brooklyn launched herself into her arms. "You're back. And you're lucky. Uncle Connor said you get to live here forever."

"I do. I just need to find a place to live. Luckily, I got the cottage next door to live in for the next month. That will give me time to find a place."

Megan hugged her. "Welcome home." She looked over at Connor. "You've made my brother a very happy man."

Her gaze met Connor's. "He makes me happy too."

"Okay, it's my turn now." Connor winked. He came over and wrapped her in a hug, kissing her thoroughly. Brooklyn's exaggerated groan made Amanda laugh as she pulled away.

"Ugh, Uncle Connor. Are you going to start kissing her all the time now?"

"I plan to, Princess. I plan to." He grinned, his eyes twinkling with unabashed happiness.

"I've got no complaints." She smiled up at him.

She felt a profound sense of belonging as they all sat down for dinner. For the first time in a very long time, she felt like she was sitting down for a family meal. Megan and Connor's playful banter filled the air, their sibling rapport evident in the way they teased each other with effortless ease. Brooklyn entertained them with wild stories about how she wanted to ride a sea horse.

Beneath the table, Connor's hand found hers, intertwining their fingers. The simple gesture sent warmth blossoming through her. His smile was quick and often, so different from when she'd first met him. He had an ease about him now.

Megan rose from her seat, gathering up dishes. "You go walk Amanda to her cottage.

I'm going to clean up." Megan turned to her. "I filled your fridge with some supplies, and there's freshly roasted coffee for tomorrow."

"Thank you. That was sweet."

"Of course. We're all truly thrilled to have you back here." Megan hugged her.

Contentment washed over her as Connor took her hand and they walked the familiar pathway to the neighboring cottage. "It feels so right to be back here."

"It feels right to have you back here."

"I've got to find a permanent place to live though."

"About that." Connor shifted nervously from one foot to the other. "You're an amazing woman, Amanda Kingston, and I'm so glad you came to Magnolia. You've changed my life. In a really good way."

"I feel like I'm different since I met you too." Her heart swelled with happiness and a sense of belonging at his words.

"How would you like to… live with me?" He frowned. "No, not that. I'm messing this up." He dropped to one knee. "Amanda Kingston, would you marry me and make me the happiest man on the planet?"

Surprise and joy surged through her as tears

began making hot trails on her cheeks. "Yes, I'll marry you. Yes. Yes."

He jumped up and swept her into his arms, twirling her around on the deck. He set her down abruptly. "Oh wait, I messed up again." He dropped to his knee once more and held out a ring box. "I was supposed to show you this when I asked you."

A single solitaire diamond sparkled in a simple gold setting. "Oh, it's beautiful."

He stood up and slipped it onto her finger. "Not as beautiful as you. And we're going to have a beautiful life together." He tenderly brushed away her tears.

"We are." She was certain they would.

A little voice piped up from behind the palm bushes lining the deck. "Uncle Connor, did she say yes?"

"She did, Princess." Connor threw his head back and laughed.

"Brooklyn Dempsey, you get back here right this minute and leave them alone," Megan called out.

"Momma, she said yes." Brooklyn raced across the sand back toward Connor's, her voice carrying over the distance.

"Congrats, you two. Welcome to the family, Amanda." Megan called out again.

"I guess you've got a readymade family, too." He grinned at her.

"Couldn't ask for a better one."

And here she was. Living the life she wanted to live. Where she wanted to live. With a man she loved and a new family.

Who knew that when her parents had brought her to Magnolia Key all those years ago, it would lead her right back here where she belonged?

~

Dear Reader

Thank you for reading my stories. I hope you enjoyed this addition to the Magnolia Key series. Next up is Tidal Treasures.

Tidal Treasures:

A woman desperate for a fresh start. A chance discovery. And a journey that could change everything.

When Jenna buys an old cottage on Magnolia Key, she's hoping to leave her troubled past behind. But as she peels away layers of wallpaper, she uncovers more than just dated decor—she finds a hidden box containing love letters from the 1920s.

Drawn into the mystery of star-crossed lovers from long ago, Jenna finds herself falling for Nash, the charming local contractor helping her renovate. But as she digs deeper into the island's secrets, she realizes that some mysteries are better left unsolved.

In this heartwarming tale of second chances and small-town charm, Jenna must decide if she's ready to confront the ghosts of her past and open her heart to a future filled with love and belonging.

Magnolia Key—where old secrets and new beginnings intertwine like sea grass in the coastal breeze.

As always, I thanks for reading my stories. I truly appreciate all of you. Until next time, Kay

ALSO BY KAY CORRELL

COMFORT CROSSING ~ THE SERIES

The Shop on Main - Book One

The Memory Box - Book Two

The Christmas Cottage - A Holiday Novella (Book 2.5)

The Letter - Book Three

The Christmas Scarf - A Holiday Novella (Book 3.5)

The Magnolia Cafe - Book Four

The Unexpected Wedding - Book Five

The Wedding in the Grove (crossover short story between series - Josephine and Paul from The Letter.)

LIGHTHOUSE POINT ~ THE SERIES

Wish Upon a Shell - Book One

Wedding on the Beach - Book Two

Love at the Lighthouse - Book Three

Cottage near the Point - Book Four

Return to the Island - Book Five

Bungalow by the Bay - Book Six

Christmas Comes to Lighthouse Point - Book Seven

CHARMING INN ~ Return to Lighthouse Point

One Simple Wish - Book One

Two of a Kind - Book Two

Three Little Things - Book Three

Four Short Weeks - Book Four

Five Years or So - Book Five

Six Hours Away - Book Six

Charming Christmas - Book Seven

SWEET RIVER ~ THE SERIES

A Dream to Believe in - Book One

A Memory to Cherish - Book Two

A Song to Remember - Book Three

A Time to Forgive - Book Four

A Summer of Secrets - Book Five

A Moment in the Moonlight - Book Six

MOONBEAM BAY ~ THE SERIES

The Parker Women - Book One

The Parker Cafe - Book Two

A Heather Parker Original - Book Three

The Parker Family Secret - Book Four

Grace Parker's Peach Pie - Book Five

The Perks of Being a Parker - Book Six

BLUE HERON COTTAGES ~ THE SERIES

Memories of the Beach - Book One

Walks along the Shore - Book Two

Bookshop near the Coast - Book Three

Restaurant on the Wharf - Book Four

Lilacs by the Sea - Book Five

Flower Shop on Magnolia - Book Six

Christmas by the Bay - Book Seven

Sea Glass from the Past - Book Eight

MAGNOLIA KEY ~ THE SERIES

Saltwater Sunrise - Book One

Encore Echoes - Book Two

Coastal Candlelight - Book Three

Tidal Treasures - Book Four

And more to come!

WIND CHIME BEACH ~ A stand-alone novel

INDIGO BAY ~

Sweet Days by the Bay - Kay's complete collection of stories in the Indigo Bay series

ABOUT THE AUTHOR

Kay Correll is a USA Today bestselling author of sweet, heartwarming stories that are a cross between women's fiction and contemporary romance. She is known for her charming small towns, quirky townsfolk, and the enduring strong friendships between the women in her books.

Kay splits her time between the southwest coast of Florida and the Midwest of the U.S. and can often be found out and about with her camera, taking a myriad of photographs, often incorporating them into her book covers. When not lost in her writing or photography, she can be found spending time with her ever-supportive husband, knitting, or playing with her puppies - a cavalier who is too cute for his own good and a naughty but adorable Australian shepherd. Their five boys are all grown now and while she misses the rowdy boy-noise chaos, she is thoroughly enjoying her empty nest years.

Learn more about Kay and her books at
kaycorrell.com

While you're there, sign up for her newsletter to
hear about new releases, sales, and giveaways.

WHERE TO FIND ME:
My shop: shop.kaycorrell.com
My author website: kaycorrell.com
authorcontact@kaycorrell.com

Join my Facebook Reader Group. We have lots
of fun and you'll hear about sales and new
releases first!
www.facebook.com/groups/KayCorrell/

I love to hear from my readers. Feel free to
contact me at authorcontact@kaycorrell.com

facebook.com/KayCorrellAuthor

instagram.com/kaycorrell

pinterest.com/kaycorrellauthor

amazon.com/author/kaycorrell

bookbub.com/authors/kay-correll

Made in the USA
Columbia, SC
24 October 2024